BELLADONNA
Bitter Conduct

Atropa Belladonna_L 853.

BELLADONNA
Bitter Conduct

№ 2 Dr. Josephine Plantæ Paradoxes

L.M. JORDEN

SOLIS MUNDI

Library of Congress registration TXu 2-359-223
ISBN 978-0-9838101-3-1 (Print)
ISBN 978-0-9838101-4-8 (Ebook)

SOLIS MUNDI

Flora Batava of Afbeelding en Beschrijving van Nederlandsche Gewassen, XI. Deel.,Jan Kops, Illustrator Christiann Sepp (Published 1853). Courtesy of biolib.de and commons.wikimedia.org. Colorisation and modification by L.M. Jorden.

For Nicolas, Alessandro and Tara,
with love to my brilliant stars

Dear Doctor, I have read your play,
Which is a good one in its way,
Purges the eyes, and moves the bowels,
And drenches handkerchiefs like towels
With tears that, in a flux of grief,
Afford hysterical relief
To shatter'd nerves and quicken'd pulses,
Which your catastrophe convulses...
-Lord Byron (George Gordon)

Prologue

Columbus Hospital Maternity Ward, 1921

A baby came into the world on a wintry March night, a blessed event that brought much joy to those in attendance. Little Peter wailed loudly as he took his first breaths, announcing that he was a healthy boy eager to make his mark upon the world.

The baby's Irish immigrant parents couldn't have been prouder. But such happiness wouldn't last more than a few hours.

The newborn cooed and stared at his parents with wide-eyed innocence. The parents were relieved they'd chosen a hospital birth for the safety it provided. They knew how fortunate they were; Mother Cabrini had founded this hospital with only $250 after begging for donations, her missionary sisters trained as nurses, and the wealthy patients' payments helped subsidize the wards for the poor like themselves, who couldn't afford a hospital's 'round the clock care.

The nurses took the baby from his mother's arms for his first bath. Little Peter playfully splashed the water as if giving baptism. "He'll grow up to be a priest," they laughed.

Nurse Mary then toweled and scooped up the baby to take him to the nurse's station. There she would administer the eye drops that would ward off bacterial infection.

She opened the bottle of silver nitrate solution and carefully placed a tiny drop in the corner of each of the newborn's eyes.

Little Peter began to scream and writhe in pain.

Nurse Mary frantically began rinsing the baby's eyes with clean water. Another nun heard the screams and rushed to help.

Mary examined the bottle and read the label in horror—silver nitrate 50%. The solution should have been a diluted 1%. She'd administered a blinding dose.

A doctor was called and upon entering, he immediately smelled the strong fumes. After examining little Peter, he shook his head sadly. "The baby won't survive, and his last moments will be spent in agony." He administered a strong sedative by injection.

The sisters were horrified. The hospital was supposed to alleviate the sufferings of the poor, not cause them. Mary was inconsolable, crying and wrung in a heap on the ward floor.

The other nurses were hysterical, too. Mother Superior was notified, and she came running to the nursery. After conferring with the doctor, she gathered her nuns around her.

"There is nothing that can be done for baby Peter in this world. Only a miraculous intercession can help him now."

A portrait of Mother Cabrini was carried from the rectory to the maternity ward, and placed over the baby's bassinet. A sister, with a gentle touch, pinned the benefactor's medallion on little Peter's swaddling. The sisters fervently prayed that Mother Cabrini would intercede and that their prayers would reach her, their last hope.

The doctor returned, and after examining the baby, declared him worse. Little Peter had contracted pneumonia from the noxious fumes, which had pierced his lungs and seared the fresh tissue.

The baby was not expected to live through the night.

The sisters began a vigil. They prayed to their patron, believing that she would intercede. Perhaps, at the least, she could alleviate little Peter's suffering and let him die in peace.

The next morning, Mrs. Smith awoke in a damp sweat. She was exhausted from the previous 24 hours—the high of a birth with all its promise, to the low of finding her newborn barely breathing and with thick bandages over his eyes.

She inched over to her son's crib, afraid to find him still.

But he was breathing on his own.

"Saints be praised, he's still with us," she told her husband. "I can at least hold his tiny hand."

The doctor was called, and declared that respiratory therapy could be stopped; the baby's lungs were now mysteriously clear. He then lifted the bandages over the baby's eyes, but found them still thickly crusted.

He turned to Mrs. Smith and shook his head. "He'll live, but I'm afraid he'll be blind."

Mrs. Smith despaired, unable to hold back her tears as she cradled her newborn in her arms and nursed him. She whispered in his ear, "I'll be your eyes, and I'll always take care of you. You're my little angel."

The doctor conferred with the Mother Superior, who then approached Mrs. Smith.

"I'm so sorry," she told the mother. "But please, you must pray with us. He's getting better—we must not give up."

"But I'm too angry. He's blind! How could this have happened?"

"You have only to give up your anger. We need everyone to pray through Mother Cabrini and believe Peter will be healed."

The vigil continued all the next day and night at baby Peter's bedside.

The following morning, the doctor arrived to examine the baby. He removed the bandages. "Well, I've never seen anything like it!" he exclaimed.

The little baby's blue eyes were crystal clear, and he blinked and followed the doctor's finger as it moved from side to side.

All signs of the blinding were gone, save for a small scar on the baby's cheek.

Mr. Smith and his family shouted in joy, and Mrs. Smith kissed and hugged her baby as if she would never let go.

"Maybe he wasn't really blinded after all?" she asked.

"But we all saw the damage," her husband responded.

Mother Superior placed a calm hand on each of Mrs. Smith's and Nurse Mary's shoulders, and breathed deeply.

She nodded towards Mother Cabrini's portrait. The woman's ethereal light blue eyes seemed to come alive from deep within the painting.

September 1935

The summer and fall of 1935 saw the pre-war situation deteriorate: the United States passed the Neutrality Act in July, with the aim of keeping the United States out of any coming war; Nazi Germany passed the racist Nuremberg Laws in September; and Mussolini was determined to invade Ethiopia on October 3rd, despite warnings of sanctions from the League of Nations.

Players

Josephine Reva, Homeopath M.D., the first woman doctor in areas of Brooklyn

Dr. Charles "Saltzie" Saltzman, Gastroenterologist and Josephine's beau

Dominick Abitello, Josephine's chauffeur

Maria and Antonio Colella, Italian immigrants who own the corner newsstand, and Josephine's patients

Teresa, Gianni and Chiara, their children

Sophie MacDowell, a first generation American, and her husband, **Andy**, a Scotsman, who own a grocery store and are also patients. Sophie works as Josephine's receptionist

Dr. Mabel McGrath, Dr. Josephine's new assistant doctor

Gisella and Tomasso Confitura, Italian opera stars playing Lady and Lord Capulet

Bella and Salvatore Arrabia, Italian opera stars playing Lady and Lord Montague

Freda Confitura, a soprano playing Juliet

Alberto Arrabia, a tenor playing Romeo

Friar Lawrence in Roméo et Juliette

Nurse in Roméo et Juliette

Captain Bevilacqua, Captain of the *SS Rex*

Donato Dellaguarda, First Mate of the *SS Rex*

Cardinal Schlummer, a Vatican cardinal

Father Della Pietra, the Devil's Advocate

Henrietta Porter-Graves, a New York socialite
Dr. Olivia Porter-Graves, Henrietta's daughter
Ernesto Cacciavolpe, a Mussolini official
Isabella Schiavone, a fashion designer
Fernando Delitto, a surreal artist
Sir Lucian Jones, a British diplomat from Gibraltar
Dr. Karl Mahlberg, the ship's doctor
A **Porter** aboard the *SS Rex*

Chapter 1 - Murder at the Opera

Thy drugs are quick. Thus with a kiss I die.
-Romeo and Juliet by William Shakespeare

J osephine, please take off that hat—I can barely see the stage." Dr.
Charles Saltzman batted at a faux ostrich feather, brushing it away
from his face.

"A lady doesn't remove her hat in public, Saltzie," Josephine
replied. "Not in Brooklyn, anyway. But I'll do my best."

She adjusted her extravagant hat, turning the brim upward at an
oblique angle. She smoothed her raven hair behind her exposed ear,
and pulled off a borrowed pearl earring so she could rest her head
comfortably against Saltzie's shoulder.

Isn't that what a gal is supposed to do? She'd studied the movie star
Katherine Hepburn seductively leaning towards her co-stars.
Josephine was a career girl, too—a medical doctor. She'd studied
anatomy and physiology, and the biology of how the mating ritual
was performed.

But she had no idea how to act on a date.

"That's better, I—" Saltzie sputtered as the ebullient feather had a
mind of its own and danced right into his mouth.

Josephine couldn't help laughing, her blue eyes twinkling behind
her wire-rimmed glasses.

"I was going to kiss you," he grimaced.

"Not so fast—it's only a date."

"Are you refusing a doctor's orders?"

Josephine whipped an Rx pad out of the pocket of her silk evening dress. "My orders, you mean?"

"A dominant female of the medical species," Saltzie conceded. He caught the buoyant feather and pushed it out of the way, looking at her expectantly.

Josephine had watched enough movies to know that she should lift her mouth to his. She removed her glasses. Without hesitation, they exchanged a quick kiss.

Roméo et Juliette, a romantic French opera, perfect for our second date, she mused.

Their first date hadn't ended well six years before—a murder got in the way of their picnic.

He's been waiting for another chance with the patience of a saint. And he was persistent. It had taken him multiple efforts of sending blooming bouquets of rose varietals in all the latest specimen jars to persuade her to come out tonight.

She turned to look at Saltzie's profile. He was handsome, wearing a dinner jacket and flashy tie, as if he'd stepped out of a movie star magazine. With a high forehead, strong nose and chin, he had sleekly oiled dark brown hair and a pencil-thin mustache just like Clark Gable's. His mirthful eyes, deep brown with flecks of green and blue, were like cracked hazelnuts, and his face crinkled when he laughed, which was often.

Somehow, he'd managed to sell all his stocks before the Crash of '29, and she'd heard he was doing very well with his Gastroenterology practice.

He's fun-loving and free-spirited, quite the opposite from my serious nature. He's sure of himself, too, a competent doctor, but with just enough naughtiness to make his female patients quiver.

But Josephine was immune to his charms.

If this is an evening spent away from my patients, I'd best make the most of it. She picked up her libretto and fanned herself. She'd never been to the Brooklyn opera before. In fact, she'd been so busy with her general medical practice that she hadn't been on any dates at all. Besides, the Depression hadn't permitted such extravagances.

She'd initially declined Saltzie's offer, having no money and no time to buy a formal dress. But her patients knew how to work a fine needle, and they were eager to trade fashion and haberdashery for extra house calls.

Maria, an Italian immigrant and a talented seamstress, like Josephine's mother, had sewn her the beautiful silk gown she was wearing. It was a lovely shade of lavender, constructed in a V-shaped bodice with bits of feathery organza at the shoulders. Maria said these "flutter sleeves" were the latest fashion. The dress did feel as light as a bird fluttering upon her skin, and it seemed to stay up to cover her bosom as if by magic.

"Your bosom, *il seno,* itsa *ampio,* ample," Maria had said admiringly, while adding a few battens. "Dontcha move too much, or the dress'll slip low and you'll really catcha his attention."

"Goodness, that's risky," Josephine had protested. She'd insisted on adding some straps.

"You don'ta like real featers, 'cause tey kill beautiful birds, so I asked te millner for faux ones. I wanna embroider te neckline wit flowers. Letsa go choose some you like."

They'd entered the glass atrium in Josephine's laboratory filled with her collection of poisonous plants: *Aconitum napellus, Digitalis purpurea, Helleborus niger* and more. She compounded the leaves, roots, stems, seeds and petals into homeopathic remedies—her 'poison cures', as she called them.

Josephine stopped at the *Atropa belladonna,* which was blooming and fruiting. *This one looks perfect.*

She reached for a sprig of the purple bursting buds and grabbed a handful of the richly dark berries. She put them in a glass bowl for Maria to model her needlework.

"Don't worry. They can't harm you if you don't eat them. But they're highly toxic, and paradoxically, they're also highly curative. Good for fevers and headaches."

"*Stai attenta!* Be careful! We can't have you die before your date. Saturday maybe itsa your last chance."

Maria never ceased to remind Josephine that she wasn't getting any younger.

"Too many young men killed in tat war," she said sadly. "The pickin's are *pochi*, little. You'da better hurry up and get married to tat doctor—you're almost 33 years old!"

She stressed the number like a prison sentence.

Josephine frowned. "I've no intention of marrying anyone."

"We'll see about tat. Letsa get the rest of your measurements."

When Maria presented the finished gown, Josephine was astounded. A soft lavender cloud of silk with embroidered leaves, berries and buds sewn around the scooped neckline. Josephine thought the neckline a little low, but said nothing.

"It's exquisite, Maria, thank you. But it's so delicate. How am I supposed to sit down? I'm used to wearing a house dress or pants under my white lab coat."

"You do like tat new fashion wearing pants. I nevva' imagined women woulda start lookin' lik'a men and showing their tuchus!"

"I climb stairs on house calls, so pants are very practical."

"None of tat! Tonight you'll be *una bella donna,* a beautiful woman."

Sophie, another patient and also the office receptionist, had loaned Josephine a pair of silk stockings and sparkling heeled shoes. She'd then permed Josephine's straight black hair into soft waves, and pinned it expertly at the nape of her neck.

The ladies had outlined Josephine's best feature, her striking celestial blue eyes, with black eyeliner. Josephine's left eye was smaller and necessitated her wearing glasses; she thought it a charming defect that helped her relate better to her patients. They were in as much medical need as she, and sooner or later, who doesn't have a disability or need to take care of another?

"Please take offa your glasses when you look into his eyes," Maria advised, nonetheless.

Lastly, the ladies contoured Josephine's face in a concoction of translucent powders and rouges. Sophie asked Josephine to pucker her lips and dabbed on deep red color.

"Good practice for kissing," they giggled.

When the ladies were done, Josephine did a double take upon seeing her reflection in the mirror.

"No more Doctor Reva," Sophie said.

"Hello p*rincipessa,* princess," Maria smiled.

"I'm in no need of any prince," Josephine protested.

"Under that lab coat you've got a nice shape," Sophie prodded Josephine's hips. "I'll bet you'll see some action tonight."

At the opera, Josephine uncomfortably smoothed her flowing silk dress around her, and smiled at Saltzie nervously. *What exactly was supposed to happen on a date—and afterwards?* She'd gotten to second, then rounded third base with Saltzie six years before, but that was in the excitement of fleeing the law. She wondered if tonight's date would lead to a home run? She knew what that meant in medical terminology. *I may as well enjoy the show, and worry about any "action" later.*

Josephine put on her glasses to look around the opera house.

What a magnificent spectacle!

The ornate theatre was framed by gilded arches and thick red brocade curtains, and the set was painted like a Veronese mansion. A live orchestra was playing in the pit below.

The opera was building to a climax in Act IV, and the scene was Juliet's bedchamber. Onstage, the beautiful diva sang with passion, questioning her resolve to fall into a deep, death-like sleep. Would she ever wake up to run away with Romeo?

"She'd be a fool to drink Friar Lawrence's potion," Josephine whispered to Saltzie. "She'll put herself into a coma."

I'd never do anything to jeopardize my life—nor my career—for love.

"It says here that the poison is Belladonna, and we know how deadly that is," Saltzie pointed to the libretto. "Remember how we used to pick the berries for our dilutions?"

"I do," replied Josephine. "They looked so delicious, as if tempting us not to eat them. It'd be easy to make that mistake."

They turned back to the stage. Juliet wore only a sheer nightgown clinging to her nude body underneath. Her damp skin glistened in the stage lights, and her long dark hair fell about her hourglass form, barely covering her modesty.

"*Bella donna* means beautiful woman in Italian, right?" Saltzie asked. Josephine nodded. "Well, tonight, you're even more of a *bella donna* than Juliet."

"Thank you, Saltzie. But I advise you not to compare *corpus voluptuous*," Josephine teased. "And I'd say Juliet is something of an exhibitionist."

Saltzie smiled. "That gives me ideas." He blew the fluff of organza sleeve away and tugged on the spaghetti strap holding up Josephine's dress. "After the show, your place or mine? We can pick up where we left off last time."

He twisted his body to embrace her, but his shin struck something hard.

"Ouch!" He gasped in pain. "Couldn't you have left that at home?" His shin had struck Josephine's surgical bag.

"But there could be a medical emergency this very evening."

Josephine hadn't needed to borrow Maria's pearl evening bag, not when she had her kit filled with precision scalpels, tourniquets and injection needles.

"Isn't your new assistant on call tonight?" Saltzie winced, rubbing his shin.

"Yes, she is. She's a capable doctor, and just completed her internship. Jobs are hard to come by for female doctors, so she was happy to work for so little pay."

Juliet's song called them back to the opera stage.

The soprano continued her solo, the indecision and fear in her voice enthralling her audience. They, too, looked captivated by her dilemma— drink the poison or not?

Josephine looked at Saltzie—was that a tear in the corner of his eye? He pulled out a monogrammed handkerchief from his pocket— Josephine noted the ostentatious letters *CAS* for Charles Albert Saltzman—and offered it first to her. When she declined, he dabbed his eyes.

The diva ran to her dressing table and picked up a large silver-framed mirror, singing to her reflection as if enchanted by the spell of her own beauty. She then jumped on her bed, and, in a whirlwind of crescendos and high C's, raised the glass bottle with both hands aloft, ready to swallow the poisonous liquid.

Juliet's operatic song seemed to fill the theater, echoing to the rafters above and making the glass chandeliers shake.

What a powerful diaphragm! Josephine was impressed.

The diva was hitting every note possible in the human scale. Josephine's mother, Grace, had been an opera singer, and together they'd sung along to recordings of famous sopranos like Nellie Melba in her duets with Enrico Caruso. After Grace died, the nuns in the orphanage had cranked the old Victrola and filled the halls with Verdi and Puccini to help Josephine mourn.

But nothing could prepare Josephine for this—her first live opera performance. The diva's divine voice filled the theatre and seemed to float on sound waves of its own.

The orchestra sounded several ominous drum rolls, as Juliet brought the crystal bottle down to her lips.

Josephine gripped Saltzie's arm. "It's incredible!"

"Indeed."

"No, I mean it's truly incredible—as in *not credible*. No poison would cause a death-like coma from which one would awaken after 48 hours."

"It's an opera based on a 400-year-old play," Saltzie noted. "It's not modern science."

Don't drink it, Juliet, Josephine whispered under her breath, shivering.

Saltzie took the opportunity to put his arm around her shoulders, and the sensation of his body heat tingled her senses.

"Isn't it romantic, Josephine?" Saltzie asked. "Wouldn't you take a drug to elope with me? I'd like to think so."

"Think again!"

Saltzie had been part of the Upper East Side Yorkvillain gang—fellow students who teased Josephine mercilessly when she was the only girl in their medical school classes. They even gave her a boy's nickname, Joe, which, unfortunately had stuck with her. But Saltzie had often come to her aid. Once during autopsy class, when the boys blocked her from getting near the cadaver (whining that a girl shouldn't examine a naked man's bits), Saltzie had encouraged her to step forward with his saucy wink. She'd then wielded her scalpel confidently to slice open the cadaver.

Maybe Saltzie was like those altar boys who used to steal coins from the church donation plate, but later became priests. Nine years had passed since medical school, and maybe it was time to forgive him.

Saltzie's hand was tenderly caressing hers while he stared at the stage. *He does love me,* she reasoned, *and I feel something when I'm around him. Love surely is a reflex, like getting banged on the knee—you can't help jerking.*

Saltzie wasn't the most honest man, Josephine had to admit. In fact, after the disaster of their first date, he'd been arrested in a bootlegging sting. But somehow he was never sentenced to prison time.

If the judge could forgive him, surely I can, too.

Most New Yorkers had no trouble forgiving him, either —his notoriety and handsome front-page photo had brought patients running to his doorstep. Saltzie now owned the most lucrative and modernly equipped gastroenterology clinic on the Upper East Side of Manhattan.

He has five doctors working under him!

Josephine fingered the large pearl necklace at her throat. A gift from Saltzie. *Should I have accepted it?*

Criminals could be reformed. After all, she'd picked a few pockets as an orphan, and even gambled for streetcar fare—both necessary vices to survive as an orphan on the streets of New York City. "Everyone deserves a second chance," Mother Cabrini had told her at the orphanage.

Josephine had been sure to seize hers.

She'd talked her way into a medical scholarship at the New York City College of Homeopathic Medicine. Despite suffering teasing and pranks by those *Yorkvillains*, she'd graduated as a homeopath with a full M.D. diploma, even taking a first in Physiology.

But no hospitals would hire a female, so Josephine left Manhattan and hung her shingle in faraway Brooklyn as the first woman doctor in Bensonhurst, Borough Park and parts of Gravesend, and built a successful practice from scratch. She now was a highly respected G.P. with hundreds of patients, treating everything from broken bones to births to illnesses to minor surgeries. Dominick, her brawny and handsome chauffeur, rushed her to the hospital, house calls and accidents.

The sight of the petite Dr. Josephine Reva walking the streets at all hours of the night in her white lab coat and carrying her black medical bag no longer alarmed most Brooklynites. The local bookies even sold odds on her survival rates (they sold odds on most anything.)

Still, most of Josephine's patients were female and pregnant. She liked to think they came to her because of her obstetrics skill, but she knew that many preferred to have another woman deliver their babies —it was slightly less embarrassing.

Having children of her own held no appeal for Josephine; she preferred to assist others in this medical miracle. In fact, she hadn't yet had sex, although she'd come close with Saltzie on their last date.

I suppose I should be enjoying this date, but why don't I feel pleasure? I've a feeling something bad is going to happen.

Saltzie's hands were now moving as fast as a surgeon's during an operation. His fingers were caressing any bare flesh he could find, and with Maria's dress there was a lot of that. He was touching most intimately her shoulders, stroking the underside of her arm and lightly flitting around the exposed contour of her breast under her sleeve. She felt a pleasant alertness all over.

Nothing's wrong, everything's going well.

Tilting her hat further to the side, she let herself fall again against Saltzie's broad chest. She ventured to nonchalantly rest her hand on his upper leg, noticing how firm his quadricep thigh muscle felt.

He reached for her hand in return, squeezing it and moving it several inches upwards. She felt his hardness and remembered him anatomically, that night she had seen him naked standing before his bed. It was at their hide-out in his waterfront cottage on Coney Island. Fortunately, they'd been interrupted by that Chief Detective O'Malley. Or perhaps, unfortunately—the foreplay hadn't seemed so bad at all.

Josephine removed her glasses and looked into Saltzie's eyes. She batted her baby blues at him. (She'd learned how to hold a man's stare from watching Miss Hepburn). He breathed deeply and she, too, felt a rush of excitement.

Tonight, I'll invite him into my laboratory for an after the opera drink. Then, who knows?

Saltzie forgot all about the gorgeous diva onstage. He only had eyes for Josephine, until the diva's ear-splitting high C brought their attention back to the stage.

Saltzie's hand abruptly dropped back to his lap. Josephine breathed a sigh of relief that the touching hadn't gone any further, and returned her focus to the opera.

"The diva is practically naked and soaked to the skin. She'll risk a serious illness." Josephine shook her head.

"Uh, huh," Saltzie said, still mesmerized by Josephine's blue eyes.

My mother, if she were alive, would surely disapprove of Juliet's technique, Josephine thought. *The high notes seem to emanate from the vocal cords in the throat instead of deeper.* Grace used to tell stories about her aristocratic childhood in the family's villa high in the cool hills overlooking Naples Bay. The opera lessons when Grace had dressed like a starlet, with silk shawls, feather hats, pearls and jewels. Of course, she'd had many suitors. But a scandal in the family had caused Grace to be deemed "un-marriageable", and packed off on a steamer ship to a supposedly rich cousin in New York. The cousin had no fortune, and nothing to offer Grace but a dingy tenement apartment and work as a seamstress in a sweat shop. A loveless marriage to a dock worker and five children later, Grace caught tuberculosis and died during the Spanish Flu epidemic. Josephine had been forced to steal on the streets for food for her siblings, until the orphanage nuns took them in.

They'd educated her, even in Latin so she could read High Mass. "You're a smart one," they told her, "even if you're nothing but a street waif." She announced defiantly that she would become a doctor —if she couldn't save her mother, she was determined to save others. "Girls don't become doctors," the nuns patted her on the head, "but you'd make a fine nurse." Only Mother Cabrini had smiled and nodded confidently.

Onstage, Juliet finally made her decision. With a most dramatic thrusting of the poison bottle up and down—clearly to enthrall the audience, thought Josephine—Juliet brought the bottle to her lips. Culminating in an extremely high-pitched note that surely broke a glass somewhere, Juliet gulped down the dark liquid.

Josephine shivered involuntarily.

"She's taking a swig," said Saltzie, "a really big swig!"

"The dose makes the poison."

"Is that Shakespeare?"

"*Dosis sola facit venenum —Paracelsus, 1493-1541.*"

"Oh, you're right, Joe. You were always the best student in class." He squeezed her hand. "I was too busy having fun with the boys."

They looked back to the stage, where the beautiful Juliet had collapsed on her bed, still as death.

The stage went dark.

"That was moving," said Saltzie. "The lovers will die in each other's arms, immortalized posthumously."

"Preposterously is more like it," huffed Josephine.

The stage lights illuminated and the next scene began.

Juliet's bedroom was now bathed in soft morning light. Lord and Lady Capulet and Juliet's nurse were weeping at the young girl's feet. Juliet lay motionless on her bed.

Her family prepared to carry her body to the Capulet tomb. Lady Capulet took center stage and began to sing a moving dirge.

But Juliet suddenly sat up. Lady Capulet looked annoyed to be interrupted. The young diva jumped up on her bed and then swung around the bedposts as if on a merry go 'round, then jumped down, pulling at the curtains and exposing the stage ropes hidden behind. The Capulets tried to catch Juliet as she flew by. The nurse look mortified and ran offstage.

"She's not supposed to be up, is she?" Josephine asked her beau. "If she's in a coma—"

"Look! She's now marching with her legs high, or is that goose stepping?" Saltzie pointed. "And it sounds like she's singing gibberish."

"What on earth?" Josephine exclaimed. "That's Italian."

"Isn't this opera in French?"

"I think it's a dialect—it's *Napolitano.*"

"Can you understand that? What's she singing about?"

"Well, it's not about Romeo. She's singing about her love for some other man. Go figure."

"Maybe we've switched to *Rigoletto*?"

Josephine looked through Saltzie's opera glasses.

"She's expanding her chest, breathing from the diaphragm, and her inhalations are full of oxygen. I've never heard such lustrous notes. I wonder how her vocal chords are holding out."

They watched Juliet strut about the stage and give several odd-looking salutes with her arm held straight out.

"What's she singing about now?"

"I can't make out every word," Josephine said. "But the refrain is *Mare Nostrum*."

"That's Latin for 'Our Sea'. We doctors learned enough of that dead language." Saltzie was intrigued. "What's the sea got to do with Romeo and Juliet? I thought they were on land, or 'on the hard', as we yachtsman say."

"*Mare Nostrum*," Josephine repeated slowly. "Isn't that a Roman emperor's slogan? He dreamed of ruling over the entire Mediterranean Sea."

"The Romans? Aren't we in Verona? Good grief!"

"Now she's wavering like a drunk!"

"Prohibition's over, so maybe the girl had a few too many?"

"Or maybe Friar Lawrence spiked her bottle with whiskey?"

"She's holding her head, as if she has a headache. Maybe she's forgotten her lines?"

Josephine handed Saltzie the opera glasses. "Saltzie, look closely at her face. She's staring wild-eyed and crying tears. Now she's flailing her arms about and gasping. I think she's in distress."

Josephine reached for her medical bag and pulled out her stethoscope, slinging it around her neck. "Let's go!"

"Now dear Joe, stop working for one evening. Try to enjoy the performance, no matter how avant-garde it is."

Josephine reluctantly sat back down.

The Capulets began pushing Juliet towards the bed, then forcefully holding her down.

"Lady Capulet looks angry," said Saltzie. "Juliet ruined her solo."

The opera stars pretended to mourn over a struggling and combative Juliet.

"She's wide awake and keeps popping upright. I'd better go check on her."

"Don't worry, Josephine, I'm sure it's all part of the opera. Maybe it's Brooklyn Bauhaus or something."

Suddenly, the stage curtain fell abruptly. All was black for a few minutes, until dimmed house lights softly illuminated the theatre. The audience murmured. A few people clapped.

"Well, that was unconventional," Saltzie said. "So let's be unconventional, too." He reached for Josephine, remembering to push the ostrich feather and the medical bag to the side. He began nuzzling Josephine's neck. "We've got an extra intermission. Where were we?"

"Saltzie, please, not now. Something's wrong. I know it."

Josephine clutched at her medical bag. "Listen! Backstage. That's Juliet shouting and making a complete fool of herself. It sounds like she's vomiting."

"Goodness, in public! That's disgusting. I'll never take another drink as long as I live."

"You'd better not. That's what landed you in jail last time."

"That was six years ago, and I haven't overstepped since."

"You mean, because Prohibition ended, there's no money in it anymore?"

"Ha, ha! Surely you jest. I'm older, wiser, and I'd never flout the law again," Saltzie said. "I've a good practice, and I make oodles of money. Why, we could go to the opera every Saturday night, and I could buy you more of these delightful dresses. And we could go to Paris, London, even Verona, anywhere your heart desires."

He pulled Josephine toward him and held her tightly. "We'd make a fine couple, Dr. and Mrs. Saltzman."

In the reflection of the chandelier, Josephine could see Saltzie's multi-colored irises flash like reflections on the water. *Was this a proposal? Should she dive in?*

"You mean Dr. and Dr. Saltzman."

She'd have to change the name plate on her office door. But to see her own name, 'Dr. Josephine Reva, MD', always filled her with such pride.

"A bee is drawn to honey," Saltzie said, as he nuzzled her neck.

The male honeybee, Josephine mused, *who buzzes to the female and mates in mid-flight.* She had done lots of research on insect reproduction in medical school. *Saltzie probably doesn't know that the male honeybee dies shortly after sex, with its reproductive organ ripped from its body.*

There was no doubting the chemistry that drew their bodies closer. She let him fold her into his arms, and eagerly lifted her mouth to his. Sparks seemed to ignite between their bodies.

"Well, as long as I'm Queen Bee." Josephine cooed while Saltzie nuzzled her more.

Besides, no one else is beating a path to my door. Probably because Josephine didn't have that "It" factor, sex appeal, and she didn't want any children. Saltzie didn't want children either—he was still something of a child himself.

"You can keep working, Joe," Saltzie whispered. He knew that would please her.

"As if any man could stop me."

"How modern!" Saltzie said. "I love a gal who knows her own mind."

His hand reached underneath her dress, touching her legs. His other hand seemed to accidentally brush her nipple through the silk as he pulled her towards him.

In turn, she reached down and stroked his thigh again, making him moan. The two kissed passionately.

"Hey, get a room!" A man in the audience yelled at the pair.

Josephine had gotten carried away. She realized the impropriety, and quickly pushed Saltzie's hands away. "You're taking liberties!"

"So were you." They moved apart.

He took her hands in his. "Listen here, I want to marry you. You can trust me."

"The last time I trusted you, you stole my purse and left me to get arrested by that Detective O'Malley."

"But I only did that to save you! I couldn't let you be accused of those Aconite murders. Remember, I orchestrated your jail break."

"Oh, how noble, coming from a prisoner." Josephine harrumphed.

"Well, what can I say? Every man has his vice." Saltzie leaned back and reached into his evening jacket, pulling out a fancy silver monogrammed cigarette case and a box of matches. The phosphorous glow from the struck match illuminated his chiseled jawline. He sucked hard on the cigarette.

"Smoking is prohibited. Didn't you read the sign?"

"Everyone is smoking anyway." He motioned around the theatre. Other audience members were taking advantage of the unplanned intermission. "I've repented, you have my word. I'll never drink another drop of whiskey."

Josephine relented. "I might let you have a few sips of champagne and smoke a few cigarillos."

"You drive a hard bargain. I need a domineering wife," he said, blowing smoke rings. "A rose by any other name smells so keen, but you're so thorny, my Josephine."

"First, I smell of antiseptic. And second, is that bad poem supposed to entice me?"

"Did it?" He leaned towards her.

"Hey, watch out for my stethoscope," she said. "And don't step on my medical bag again. It's expensive."

"Love's true course never did run smoothly." He retreated.

Josephine felt a touch of remorse, remembering what Maria had said. This marriage proposal could be her last chance, and she wasn't getting any younger. Had she blown her opportunity? She decided to lean forward to give him a peck on the cheek.

"Do I take it that kiss means yes?"

"I'm thinking about it," she answered.

Saltzie delightedly blew more smoke rings.

"I suppose you'd like a proper proposal, with a grand gesture in some romantic place, not a dark theatre."

"Is that what you wanted by asking me to change my professional name?" she bristled.

"There are those thorns again."

"I thought it was my thorny exterior you waxed poetic about."

"Indeed. Let's take a good look at that exterior."

Josephine laughed, smoothing the silk.

"Perhaps I should give you an examination," he said.

"I could say the very same thing to you."

"Please do! Let's play doctor."

He leaned forward to kiss her lips, but she had turned her head and he got a mouthful of ostrich feather instead.

"Darn! That blasted hat!"

"It's one of my patient's latest creations. Isn't it lovely? They're so thoughtful."

"Must we talk about your patients? Well, so much for a romantic night at the opera," Saltzie said, sulking in his seat. "I wonder what's next?"

The curtain lifted and the final act began.

The setting was inside the Capulet tomb and Juliet was lying motionless on the slab.

"Looks like this trolley is back on its tracks," Saltzie laughed. "Dr. Reva, you can put your stethoscope away."

Josephine kept her stethoscope on. If anything, it would keep Saltzie's hands off her chest.

"Here comes Romeo," Josephine pointed to stage right. "He could go into shock."

Romeo began his solo, his sonorous and booming tenor wailing in grief. Josephine was transported by his song.

Romeo drank from the poison bottle he brought with him. He stumbled about for a dramatic ten minutes in his death throes, singing his solo and reaching for Juliet.

Then he stopped singing. He seemed to be waiting.

The music also stopped—the conductor in the pit stood like a statue with his baton poised in mid-air.

There was an awkward silence in the opera house. Josephine could hear the glass chandeliers clinking.

She checked the libretto.

"It says here that Juliet is supposed to wake up now."

"What the devil is she doing? She's still lying there."

Josephine turned some pages. "Juliet awakens, then they kiss and sing a final lover's duet together."

"Hey, that's not right. In Shakespeare, Juliet's not supposed to wake up until after Romeo is dead."

"That's not how the opera goes. Look here." She pointed to the libretto. "It's topsy turvy. The composer added an extra duet with both lovers alive, then has them dying together—maybe he thought that would sell more tickets?"

"Shakespeare's rolling over in his grave."

"Get up, Juliet!" a heckler shouted. A Brooklyn audience wasn't afraid to make its frustrations known.

"We're waiting for your duet!" another blurted out.

"The libretto—" Josephine began. "Oh! *fuggetabuttit!*"

Romeo lay back down next to Juliet, who still was inert.

"What's happening?" someone in the audience shouted.

"Time to march around some more, Juliet," another voice chortled.

There was a resounding chorus of Brooklyn boos.

"I think they're killing themselves because this opera is so bad," someone shouted. Laughter filled the opera house.

"Well she isn't really dead. We're no fools," Josephine said.

Most of the ensemble were waiting in the wings, peering out from behind the curtains and looking confused. Lord Montague started to walk onstage, then realized he hadn't received his cue. Lord and Lady Capulet began pacing, peering around the curtain every few seconds.

Lady Capulet took control and signaled to the orchestra pit.

The conductor whipped his baton, and the music started again. But Juliet did not arise from the slab to sing.

Josephine took the opera glasses. She could see Romeo poking at Juliet's body.

"She wouldn't go on the slab, and now she won't get off it!" Saltzie heckled. The audience erupted in laughter.

"Saltzie! Show some sympathy! Something could be wrong with Juliet," Josephine said.

Romeo frantically signaled to the conductor to stop the music.

Then, he began shouting in Italian, which Josephine understood. *"Freda? Dai, alzati! Devi cantare! Stai addormentando? Svegliati!* Freda? Get up! It's your number. Are you sleeping? Wake up!"

The tenor gave up and started singing the final love duet alone. He moved into position and held out his arms for a Juliet who wasn't there. Then he moved to the opposite side to sing Juliet's part. His voice cracked a few times, reaching for soprano notes. He stretched out his arms, embracing himself, reminding Josephine of a pair of contorting flamingoes entwining their long necks. The audience erupted in laughter.

"He doesn't look like a soprano, nor sound like one. Maybe a castrato." Saltzie laughed.

"Look! He's taken her arm and is using it to stab her body with the dagger, trying to make it look as though—"

Romeo gave a dramatic death spiral, with several crescendos of his booming voice, and fell upon Juliet.

Josephine looked through the opera glasses again. Romeo poked Juliet's body more forcefully. Then he crept up her body and placed his hand over her heart, then over her mouth.

Suddenly, Romeo's face twisted in a mask of anguish.

He cried out: *"MEDICO! AIUTACI!"*

Josephine understood. The tenor had asked if there was a doctor in the house.

She stood up, grabbing her medical bag.

"Saltzie, come on! He's called for a doctor. Something's wrong with Juliet."

The two rushed down the aisle. "Make way!" Josephine called.

Saltzie hoisted Josephine up over the lights, and they both hurried towards center stage.

Chapter 2 - A True Apothecary

L ord and Lady Capulet were cradling Juliet, and the other players were slapping her face trying to revive her. Romeo was kissing her hand.

"We're doctors," Josephine shouted. "Let us through."

Romeo and the other singers stepped aside, as Josephine and Saltzie reached the prone diva.

Josephine placed her stethoscope on Juliet's chest and listened, then took her pulse. "She's still alive, thank goodness. Her heartbeat is racing. Tachycardia of 132, breathing irregular with intercostal retractions, paradoxical thorax, some abdominal movements. Breathing sounds on auscultation."

Saltzie pulled back Juliet's eyelids and shined a pen light into her pupils. "On the Glascow coma scale, a score of 7, severe."

"Pupils are isochoric, mydriatic and heavily dilated," Josephine noted. "There are signs of lacrimation."

"Pupillary light reflexes are not bilaterally intact, but her eyelids show no bilateral pitosis," Saltzie added.

"There's redness of the face and neck, dryness of oral mucosa," Josephine said worriedly. "I believe she's in toxic cholinergic shock."

"Were there any sign of hypoactive bowel sounds?" she asked Romeo. "That's stomach troubles."

"Yes," he nodded weakly.

Two men in flowing purple robes hurried over from stage right. Josephine assumed they were players in the opera. The divas and dons were similarly dressed in rich velvet cloaks in jewel tones.

"Oh, thank goodness, Cardinal, please help my daughter," Lady Capulet shrieked.

"The Signorina was a devout Catholic. It's in our hands now." The stouter priest gruffly pushed the doctors aside.

"Who do you think you are!" Saltzie said.

"I'm Cardinal Schlummer and this is Father Della Pietra. I'm Freda's confessor."

"Go away! We're trying to save her life! She doesn't need a confession at the moment." Saltzie pushed them back.

Josephine defused the situation. "Cardinal and Father, please pray over there until she's stable." The two priests relented and moved aside while Josephine and Saltzie continued working.

"There are no wounds on her body," Josephine whispered to Saltzie.

"Her respiration is getting worse."

"It looks like she's been poisoned." Josephine paused. "Possibly a botanical. Atropine, hyoscyamine or maybe hyoscine—the latter chemicals cause hallucinations and short term memory loss. We need to do a gastric lavage."

"That's your area of the *corpus humanus*. Do you have any activated charcoal?"

"Of course. I've got a packet in my medical bag. I'll get a suction going. Let's set up a stomach pump."

Josephine had all the necessary contrivances in her kit. The two worked energetically, and the diva began vomiting.

"What a smell!" exclaimed Saltzie. "It's putrid. Like rotten eggs. It's almost knocking me unconscious. I wonder what she ate."

Josephine ignored Saltzie. "If we can get her to a hospital, she may have a chance. If there's no organ damage."

"An ambulance will take too long," Saltzie said. "Quickly," he called to the stage hands. "Lift her on a plank and get her into my roadster. It's parked out front."

But Juliet suddenly lurched upright, staring blankly ahead with wide-eyed stupefaction.

She cried out, "*Amore mio!* My love!"

Josephine noticed that Juliet wasn't looking in Romeo's direction, but oddly, at the two priests. *She must have been blinded by the stage lights.*

The diva then gasped and fell back flat on the slab.

Josephine frantically moved her stethoscope against the diva's chest.

"There's no heartbeat."

"No respiration," Saltzie added, placing a doctor's mirror over the diva's mouth.

Josephine quickly reached in her medical bag and found her resuscitation bellows—an instrument she'd jerry-rigged from a leather fireplace bellows and a rubber hose. She put the edge of the hose up one of Juliet's nostrils. She then stomped on the bellows to force air into the lungs. Juliet's chest inflated.

Saltzie began pounding on Juliet's heart, then listened for a heart beat. He then repeated the blows rhythmically.

After twenty minutes of strenuous efforts, both doctors gave up. They sat down exhausted, sweating and breathing heavily.

"I'm sorry," Josephine said to the troupe. "There's nothing more we can do. She's not responding."

Lady Capulet shrieked and collapsed to the floor. Lord Capulet ran to his wife and held her tightly. Romeo was crying. Lord Montague looked confused, and Friar Lawrence looked downcast. The nurse ran off backstage.

The cardinal and priest took purple stoles from their pockets and placed them over their suits. "*Permesso,* excuse me," the cardinal brushed Saltzie and Josephine aside to perform Last Rites.

There were several gasps from the audience.

"Lower the curtain!" someone called out.

The cardinal's hands touched the dead Juliet's face, and lowered her eyelids.

"Now what?" Saltzie asked Josephine.

"We've gotta find that poison bottle, and test it," Josephine said. "I wonder which botanical poison killed Juliet and why she ingested it? Maybe then we can explain this death."

"I'm no poison expert, but Joe, you are. You solved the 'Queen of Poison' cases back in '29."

"Well, I haven't had any more Aconite poisonings since then. I've had two arsenic cases from rat poison, and lead cases from a can of old soup, and children eating paint chips falling ill, and lead make-up. Oh, there was one suicide by cyanide. But this death doesn't present like any of those."

"No, you're right. I didn't smell any bitter almonds from arsenic, nor see any trace of foaming from cyanide. It must have been a botanical."

"Juliet was suffering from delirium while marching around onstage."

"A slower acting poison that causes hallucinations and brings on an anti-cholinergic toxic syndrome."

"Aconite can cause hallucinations, and the victim sees a yellow glow."

She turned to the opera troupe. "Did Juliet say anything about seeing a strange yellow glow?" They shook their heads.

The cardinal and priest were still murmuring Last Rites

Romeo was distraught. "*Mia Freda, mi amore.* My Freda, my love," he kept wailing in despair. The Capulets were crying over Juliet's body.

"You don't think it could've been a cardiac arrest from all her exertions onstage?" Saltzie asked.

"No, the cardiac arrest came after the other symptoms. The questions we need to ask are: which botanical poison did Juliet take, and was it suicide or murder?"

"I think we'd better call the police." Saltzie motioned for a stage hand to make the call.

"Oh, no! Chief Detective O'Malley is on duty at night," said Josephine. "What if he arrests us again?"

"Don't worry. Remember, I was with you the whole time in the audience throughout the play, holding your hand. We're each other's alibi."

"Yes, of course, how could I forget?"

"I was touching you, and kissing your neck, but we don't need to tell the Detective that part."

"Saltzie, a woman has died. Be serious."

Josephine paused. "Remember how crazed Juliet became after drinking Friar Lawrence's potion? That wasn't in the libretto."

"Yes, I remember. She was making up her own aria."

"I believe she was poisoned then."

"Or perhaps the poison was in Romeo's bottle from the final scene?" Saltzie asked.

"I don't think her lips ever touched that one."

"You're so observant, like a detective. Are you sure you haven't missed your calling?"

"No, I'm happy being a simple Homeopath GP. Let's find that poison bottle. We need a sample from it—before Chief Detective O'Malley gets here. I doubt he'll test for a botanical."

They searched the bedchamber and crypt sets, but to no avail.

"It's gone," Josephine sighed. "Someone must have taken it."

There was the sound of sirens, and a bevy of blue uniformed police officers swarmed the stage.

Chapter 3 - Questioning the Suspects

T he imposing figure of Chief Detective O'Malley entered from stage left. He wore a baggy trench coat, which hung over his tall gangly frame, and underneath he wore a grey pinstriped suit, and a rumpled white shirt with the tie pulled askew. A fedora was cocked back on his head. Josephine noted that the stubble of his beard and his pallor were grayer than six years before. That was when he'd thrown her in a basement cell called "The Pit" and accused her of the Aconite murders.

He must be working 'round the clock. She noticed that his eyes were bloodshot, suggesting he hadn't slept in days.

But his grey eyes still glinted like sharpened steel.

He leaned towards Josephine like a fox tracking its prey.

"Doctor Reva, I should've guessed I'd find you here. You seem to have an affinity for death."

"Chief Detective, you're looking very tired, so I'll excuse that comment," she parried. "You must come see me for a check-up. I'm going to write you a prescription for some vitamins." She pulled out the Rx pad from the pocket of her silk gown.

"No sleep, dinners at the Automat. I'm getting too old for this line of work. Bootleggers replaced by organized crime—it's gotten even worse."

Josephine handed him the prescription.

He shrugged and pointed to the body. "Let's not discuss me, when a young woman in the prime of life is dead. And she died right in front of you. I suppose you have an alibi this time?"

"Yes, I do. And it's air tight. I was sitting in the audience when Juliet became ill."

"With me," Saltzie stepped forward and put his arm protectively around Josephine. "We're each other's alibi."

"You two just happen to be fans of opera?" The detective nodded his head from one to the other. "Oh, I see. On a date? Swell! Was it going well?"

"It was, until Juliet died," Saltzie muttered.

"Interfered with your after the opera plans?" O'Malley smirked.

The Chief Detective then ordered his men to question the troupe. He turned to Josephine and Saltzie.

"I managed to save both your necks last time with the Aconite murders, so the least you two can do is tell me exactly what happened here."

"She was singing, and drank poison onstage." Josephine knew how to get to the point.

"Friar Lawrence convinced Juliet to go into a coma so she could marry her true love Romeo against her parents' wishes," Saltzie added. "Shakespeare, you know."

"No, I don't know. Coppers don't have time to lollygag at the opera."

"Well, it's a play on misunderstandings turned tragic, like the original Romeo and Juliet—Pyramus and Thisbe in Ovid's Metamorphoses. One thought the other dead: he found her veil ripped by a lioness, so he wrongly assumed she was eaten alive, and killed himself," Josephine explained.

O'Malley looked at Josephine incredulously. "A lion? I'm not a big mythology fan. I prefer real life, so shall we continue?"

Josephine and Saltzie reluctantly nodded.

"Let me get this straight. In the play, Juliet drank some poison while onstage?"

"Yes," Saltzie said.

"Then it looks like an open and shut case to me. She wanted to die in front of her adoring fans. Suicide."

"But wait, Detective. It could be murder," Josephine began.

"Who gave her the bottle?"

"Friar Lawrence."

O"Malley called over the singer dressed in a brown monk's robe. He had heavy stage makeup on to make him look older, but he was actually no more than a youth.

"*Si, signore,*" Friar Lawrence said. "*Cosa volete?*"

"Dr. Reva, make yourself useful. Translate for me." He turned to the friar.

"You gave Juliet the potion, but did anyone else touch it?" Josephine translated the question into Italian.

The friar shook his head.

"Did you put real poison in it?" O'Malley asked.

Friar Lawrence looked alarmed. He spun on his heel and ran away towards the exit.

"Well don't just stand there!" O'Malley shouted at his men. Several officers ran off to apprehend the suspect, but the young man slipped past them.

"He's just a youth, and probably scared," Josephine said.

"Or maybe he's got a record, a juvenile delinquent."

Josephine sighed. She was sure the detective was barking up the wrong tree. But she didn't know who else might be a likely suspect.

Chief Detective O'Malley turned to his sergeant.

"Did you find any weapon?'

"Only this rubber dagger." The sergeant held up Romeo's weapon and bent it back and forth.

"Detective, there's no sign of any trauma to the body," Saltzie said.

Chief Detective O'Malley continued. "Then this looks more and more like a suicide. She killed herself."

"But it can't be suicide," Josephine stammered. "It doesn't add up. It's got to be murder."

"Really? And what makes you a better detective than me?"

Josephine looked into Chief Detective O'Malley's steely eyes.

"Detective, this poison caused a slow, lingering death—wouldn't someone wanting to commit suicide take something stronger to die quickly?"

"Who knows the mind of a suicidal person?"

If only Josephine could put her finger on some evidence. The detective continued to stare at her. Their eyes locked as if they were in a contest of wills. After a few seconds, she gave up and looked away. Chief Detective O'Malley looked pleased and strutted off to question the other opera stars.

Josephine pulled Saltzie aside and whispered to him.

"Her skin pallor was almost glowing strangely."

"You mean, like make-up?"

"It's possible. Or an overdose. Remember poison can become a homeopathic remedy, after careful dilutions, shaking and dynamizing."

"'Poison cures'—that's certainly a paradox."

"Maybe she was taking Belladonna to make her pupils bigger and her skin brighter. She seemed vain to me, singing to her own reflection. What if that bottle contained a lethal dose?"

"Could be. Goodness knows, sometimes we students got the dilutions wrong."

"Well, you may have, but I never did. I used to make each remedy by hand with Professor Heath in the laboratory."

Josephine still grew the plants, extracted them in alcohol, then diluted and "succused" them, shaking them over and over, until they were so dilute that only the ions would stimulate a person's vital force to counteract the malady. But homeopathics were now only a small part of her practice, and she was using the new sulfa drugs more.

"It is fascinating how well the homeopathic remedies work, even if many doctors don't believe in them anymore."

"Yes, hardly any doctors use homeopathics. Most doctors are prescribing stronger strengths of the new toxic drugs. They act more quickly, you know."

That's such a shame, thought Josephine. "It's the Law of Infinitesimals that makes the homeopathic remedy so powerful. *The more dilute the extract, the more potent. Ad infinitum.*

"We must cure a disease without exacerbating it or causing worse symptoms."

"'Side effects', they call them now."

"That's just another term for toxic effects—they're hardly on the side. Any ill effect is bad, no matter what you call it—"

"Not again, Miss Lady Doctor." Chief Detective O'Malley interrupted as he came towards them.

"Dr. Reva's poison plant paradoxes, your poison cures, the Laws of Similars and of Infinitesimals."

Josephine felt the need to defend her beloved botanicals.

"You know, Detective, many plants are beneficial, even if they are poisonous. Belladonna, for example, dilates the pupils and ophthalmologists use it for eye surgery; Cinchona Bark, which contains Quinine, treats malaria; and Foxglove, which contains Digitalis, restarts the heart."

"Well, I suppose so."

"But it's the dilution that gives them further strength—a homeopathic remedy is made according to the Law of—"

"—of Infinitesimals. Yes, I remember Senator Copeland, a Homeopath, explaining it to me. It's diluted over and over again, until no molecules remain, but somehow it's still activated."

"Chemistry has advanced to the point where ions are recognized to exist after molecules break apart. Through the succussion process, the ions are transferred to the surrounding water. Professor Heath said chemistry proved that Homeopathic remedies hold therapeutic value."

"Ions, transference to water—it's still a mystery to me. So did either of you give her a homeopathic dose that went wrong?"

"We're professionally trained MD's," blustered Saltzie. "We don't prescribe incorrect doses of homeopathic remedies. And we had nothing to do with this diva's death."

At that moment, the sergeant interrupted to report that the officers couldn't find any glass bottle.

Detective O'Malley closed his notebook. "We don't need it, anyway." He looked around. "We'll wait for toxicology on the corpse.

Modern methods. It still looks like an open and shut case, just the way I like 'em. Suicide."

"But Detective, don't you want to check the bottle for fingerprints?" asked Saltzie.

"I'm sure it's been smudged with Juliet's fingerprints."

The Montagues and Capulets, with their long velvet robes trailing behind them, marched over angrily.

"Detective, can't we go to our dressing rooms?" Lady Montague pulled her ermine collar up against her throat and stamped her feet. "We've been here over an hour. We must rest our voices and gargle."

"And you are?"

"Salvatore and Bella Arrabia, we play Lord and Lady Montague. And we are the mother and father of Alberto, that's Romeo."

"And who are you two?" O'Malley motioned to the other couple, who were red-eyed and crying.

"Tomasso and Gisella Confitura, Lord and Lady Capulet. We're Freda's, that's Juliet's, parents."

"Bella Arrabia, Gisella Confitura. Is that two r's and one l, or one r and two l's?" The rookie looked down at his notepad as he puzzled over the spellings. "I'm just going to list you by your Shakespearean names for now.

"Hold on a moment," O'Malley said. "You mean youz Capulets are Juliet's parents in real life, and youz Montagues are Romeo's?

"Yes," they answered.

"And I suppose you're going to tell me that Romeo and Juliet were in love, in real life?"

"Yes."

"Well, they say life is theater."

"I believe what you mean, Detective, is that life imitates art. It was Oscar Wilde—" Lord Montague interjected.

"Yes, yes, I know," Detective O'Malley cut him off. "I know my Irish poets. I'm Irish myself."

"Oh, that explains it," sniffed Lord Montague.

Chief Detective O'Malley turned back to the Capulets. "I'm sorry for your loss. Was there any reason Juliet would want to kill herself?

"Why no! She had every reason to live. She was a star, and this was her breakout role," Lady Capulet answered. "And she was in love with Alberto—that's Romeo."

"No," said Lady Montague."Well, he wasn't in love with her. It was nothing more than a fling."

"But mother, we were *absolutamente,* absolutely in love," Alberto said, as he strode defiantly over.

"You mean you planned to marry Juliet?" O'Malley asked him.

"Yes, upon our return."

"Over my dead body!" Lady Montague interjected. "She was not right for my Alberto, and her singing was, how should I say, overly dramatic."

"Mamma, you couldn't have stopped us—we were going to elope when we got back to Naples!"

"*Dio buono!* Good God! It's better she killed herself!"

"Mamma, how could you say such a thing!"

"So you wished her dead?" O'Malley asked Lady Montague.

"Are you insinuating that I killed her? No, of course not. I didn't want her to marry my son, that's all, " Lady Montague said. "Alberto's a star. He'll be more famous than Caruso!" She turned to her son. "You'll do much better as a solo act."

"How can you speak such trite when my beautiful daughter lies dead?" Lady Capulet furiously reached to slap Lady Montague, who recoiled like a spitting snake. The two tussled, tearing at their velvet robes, until their husbands pulled them apart. The women adjusted their bejeweled headbands and torn lace collars, and stood defiantly opposite each other.

"Detective, you've wasted our time long enough. We have nothing to do with the girl's death," said Lord Montague, as he tugged Lady Montague's arm to lead her away.

But he remembered to bow his head slightly to Juliet's parents. "Signori Confitura, we're deeply sorry for your loss." With that Lord and Lady Montague turned on their heels and headed backstage with a swish of their velvet robes.

"Don't leave the building." O'Malley called out to them. He eyed them and made some notes. He turned back to the Capulets.

"Do you think the Montagues, or anyone else, would have wanted to harm your daughter?

"I don't know. Bella was jealous of Freda's voice, and so were many others," moaned Lady Capulet "A coloratura soprano—my daughter had a lovely gift." She sneered in Lady Montague's direction. "One that Bella never had."

The coroner placed a sheet over Juliet. Lady Capulet wailed in despair, and Romeo ran to his lover's side to grasp her cold hand.

"Oh, she was so beautiful." Lady Capulet wept.

Lord Capulet turned and said gruffly to the detective, "Can't this wait?"

The detective nodded. The distraught Capulets walked offstage following their daughter's body carried away on a gurney.

"No love lost between those fighting families," O'Malley said to his sergeant and rookie. "Let's talk to the rest of the troupe." He pointed out two persons to Josephine and Saltzie. "Those two actors, the Papal emissaries, where were they onstage when Juliet died?"

"They really are Papal emissaries," said Josephine.

"They're not part of the opera?"

"No, life doesn't imitate that stuff about brotherly love at the Vatican," Saltzie said bitterly. "The Pope sits quietly while Hitler enacts racist laws against Jews."

Josephine introduced the two priests as Cardinal Schlummer and Father Della Pietra.

"Did you two come all the way from Rome," the Chief Detective asked, "just to perform Last Rites?"

"No," the cardinal said. "We're in New York on very important Papal business."

"What Papal business?" O'Malley asked.

"We've been sent by the Vatican to avow the miracles of Mother Cabrini. She stopped death and suffering to intercede for our Lord."

"We're here to investigate her beatification," the priest added.

"Her what?

"That's the next step. First she's venerated, then beatified before she is canonized."

"Canonized means being named a saint," the priest added. "We came to collect her relics and bring them back to Rome."

"So how did you know Juliet?"

"We were on the same ocean liner, the *SS Rex*," the cardinal continued. "I met Signorina Freda, Juliet, and the other stars on board. I heard her confession several times. Freda was a devout

Roman Catholic. I'm sure she'd have wanted me to perform the Last Rites for her."

"And did she, by any chance, make a confession or show any signs of wanting to end her life?" O'Malley asked hopefully.

"You know, Detective, the confessional is sealed. I'm not at liberty to divulge anything that Freda said to me in confidence. But she made no sign of wanting to end her life—quite the opposite. She was in love with Alberto, and they wanted me to marry them upon their return to Naples."

"And you, then?" the detective turned to the priest."Who are you?"

"I'm the Devil's Advocate,"

"And what, pray tell us, is that?

"I take the part of the Devil, to disprove the miracles. These were Satan's attempts to impersonate our most Holy One."

O'Malley was not a believer himself despite his Irish Catholic upbringing. His wife's early death had hurled him into a cynicism darker than any priest's hole.

"Did you see any Satan killing Juliet?" asked the detective.

"No, I didn't. I saw no one."

"Detective, I think she was poisoned when she drank from Friar Lawrence's potion," interrupted Josephine.

Chief Detective O'Malley started to push at his throbbing temples.

"Oh, you do, do you? Who was with the diva, if she was murdered?"

"No one was with her, she was alone onstage singing her solo," replied Josephine.

"Who was with her when she took her last breath?"

"Me, Saltzie, the Capulets, the Montagues, Romeo, the nurse, Friar Lawrence, and the Papal emisaries," said Josephine.

"Well," said O'Malley, "if, as you say, Detective Reva, it was murder, then I doubt her parents or her fiancé killed her. Nor these priests. So that leaves the Montagues, Friar Lawrence and the Nurse. Lady Montague clearly held no love for Juliet. The nurse is bawling in the corner, she's not making any sense, and Friar Lawrence has flown the coop. And you two, Saltzie and Josephine. You two have an alibi. So if it's murder, I'd bet my hat it's Friar Lawrence."

An officer returned tugging Friar Lawrence gruffly by the collar.

"I didn't do anything! I just gave her the bottle, that's all." the youth wailed, as Josephine translated.

"Take him away to the station. If he killed her, we'll make him talk."

"You can save yourself the trouble. He didn't kill her," said Josephine.

Chief Detective O'Malley turned to her and asked, "Why not?"

"It's hardly likely that Friar Lawrence poisoned Juliet when he handed her the poison in front of hundreds of people."

The detective considered that for a moment. "So Detective Reva, then who did it? The Montagues? The nurse? What's the motive?"

"I don't know that yet."

"I still think it's suicide."

"And I think it's murder!" Josephine was adamant. The two stared at each other, and this time O'Malley turned away first. He was starting to doubt his conviction.

"But you can't tell me it's not a suicide," he continued. "You heard the cardinal—Alberto and Freda were in love, but both sets of parents were not pleased about it. Plenty of lovers have troubles and kill themselves—look at Romeo and Juliet."

"Well, that's true, I suppose."

"Dr. Reva, was Juliet healthy?" the rookie asked.

"I can't really say without conducting a full medical exam, but, judging from her singing—she had good stamina, breath control and lung function. She didn't show signs of any disease, maybe only a slight cold."

"But she sang some strange verses," Saltzie added.

"Yes, that's right," Josephine said. "She started singing about her country becoming the Roman Empire again—she kept repeating *Romanitas, Mare Nostrum, vincere et vinceremo.*"

"What does that mean?

"*Mare Nostrum*, our sea, and *vincere et vinceremo* means to win, we will win."

"Those are Fascist slogans," O'Malley said.

"Remember those Fascist and Nazi Bund meetings in Brooklyn," said the sergeant. "And those Nazi camps on Long Island get thousands of Hitler lovers every weekend. We have to send officers to help the local police break 'em up."

"Yes, Hitler's Brownshirts, Mussolini's Blackshirts, and Franco's Blueshirts, and now we've got the Silvershirts—our own Fascist fanatics. They aim to take over our government with religious zealots, give the state control of private lands, enact more racist laws and deport Jews."

"Fascism is taking root in the USA, and it'll grow like a weed if news of this murder leaks," said Josephine.

"Maybe Juliet killed herself to be some kind of martyr for the Fascist cause?" the sergeant proposed.

"Josephine, didn't Juliet sing another song?" Saltzie remembered. "What was it?"

"Something about a girl from Abyssinia."

"I'll be seein' ya? What's that got to do with anything?" O'Malley asked.

"Not 'I'll be seeing ya'. Abyssinia—it's an ancient name for Ethiopia. Mussolini will soon invade it," the cardinal explained. "Preparations are under way right now."

"Why would Mussolini want to invade an African country? He'll only cause death and destruction. How horrid!" said Josephine.

"An invasion of a sovereign country could spark another world war," Chief Detective O'Malley said. "If no one stops Mussolini, that'd probably trigger the Nazis."

"Italy tried to invade Abyssinia before but they failed, leaving untold suffering for the Ethiopians," added the Devil's Advocate.

"But many Italians have never forgotten that military loss," said the cardinal. "Italian expansion is just beginning."

"It sounds like an open wound festering," said Josephine. "Mussolini's infection could spread."

"The Fascists are becoming maniacal, like the Nazis," Saltzie added. "We Jews recognize the signs."

"But Italians don't hate Jews," the rookie said. "They haven't made any laws against them."

"Not yet," Saltzie replied. "But we're always the scapegoats. All these movements, whether Hitler's Brownshirts, Mussolini's Blackshirts, Franco's Blueshirts—they have that in common."

"Yes, Saltie's right. Hitler just passed the anti-Jewish Citizenship Law," said Chief Detective O'Malley, "and that's a bad sign of worse to come from Mussolini."

"Juliet also sang something about the number fourteen," Josephine remembered. "Does that have anything to do with this?"

"That's the 14th Year of the Fascist Era. The Fascists created a new calendar to mark their election to the Senate," the cardinal explained."Year one was the first year Mussolini took power.

"So when's the 14th year of the Fascist Era?" O'Malley asked.

"That'll be next year."

"You see, she was looking forward to the future," Josephine said. "Her marriage to Alberto, Mussolini's victory in Abyssinia, the resurrection of the Italian Empire, Fascist glory. She didn't kill herself."

"For a believer like Freda, Fascism meant everything," the cardinal added.

"But her fascist beliefs were probably anathema to many," said Saltzie, unable to hide the disgust in his voice. "An anti-Fascist might've wanted her dead."

"It was murder, I just know it," said Josephine, "and her song has something to do with it."

""But the question is: would Juliet give her life for the cause? Become a martyr? Or was it murder?" asked the Chief Detective. "I'll get to the bottom of it."

He turned to his officers. "We'll question Friar Lawrence at the station. And bring the Montagues and Capulets back from their dressing rooms."

The sergeant and rookie left the stage.

Saltzie showed Josephine the libretto. "It says here that Shakespeare's poison in Romeo and Juliet was Belladonna. What if life really is imitating art?"

"Who would be so diabolical? Belladonna is a member of the Aster family. *Atropa belladonna, family Solanaceae, genus Atropa*. It's one of the deadliest botanical poisons. There's no known antidote—perhaps an anticoagulant might've helped."

"Don't fret, Josephine. There's nothing more we could have done to save poor Juliet."

"But as a homeopathic remedy, Belladonna cures high fevers and scarlet fever, stabbing and throbbing migraines. The patient presents with delirium, wildness, feels hot and cold, the face is flushed, head pains, staggers or lurches about and the pupils are dilated. Juliet exhibited these symptoms onstage."

"Yes, that's true," said Saltzie.

"We've got to find that bottle."

"Everyone in the audience can go home," O'Malley's booming voice announced. "But youz in the opera troupe, do not leave Brooklyn."

Lady Montague stomped over to him. "We sail home to Italy the day after tomorrow."

"You wanna bet?"

"We're cultural ambassadors on tour with diplomatic immunity from Mussolini himself. You can't stop us."

Chapter 4 - Brooklyn Precinct 962

*G**ood grief,* groaned O'Malley as he clapped his hand to his forehead, *fascist riots and fascist divas. I've been up all night racking my brains. Murder or martyrdom?*

He dissolved another tiny white pill of a homeopathic remedy in a glass of water for his migraine, then drank it.

What Dr. Reva said is beginning to make sense. It must be murder.

I've got to solve this case before those opera stars sail away, or there goes my Third Grade Commendation. There'll be a black mark on my record: 'Unsolved Crime.'

And someone will be getting away with murder.

He groaned again, then shouted for his men.

"Sarge, Rookie, bring in Friar Lawrence. It's time for a confession."

The officers reentered with the youth, who was shaking.

"We can't hold him any longer—not without toxicology," the rookie said. "Wickersham rules."

"Ah, yes, no officer must extract a confession with pain or force, but we don't do that, do we, boys?" He laughed sarcastically.

"Why did you poison her, Friar Lawrence? Confess!" The sergeant shouted loudly, pounding the table as he leaned in close to Friar Lawrence's face, shaking his fist.

The youth trembled. Still dressed in a monk's coarse robe, he had removed his fake bald plate and his pancake makeup was running down his face.

"I dunno," he stammered, then continued in Italian. None of the officers could understand him, so he pantomimed the sequence: a table with a bottle already on top, the Friar lifting it off the table and offering it to Juliet. "*Sono innocente!* I'm innocent!"

O'Malley sighed, remembering what Josephine had said—it was unlikely that the Friar would poison anyone in front of hundreds of spectators.

It must be one of the other opera divas or dons.

How he hated to let a murderer sail away. Especially a fascist one. News of the murder would rally Brooklyn's fascists, like setting a spark to a keg of gunpowder. The murder was surely all over the front pages of the early editions by now, and there'd be pressure to find the culprit quickly.

"I'm going to let you go, on one condition: you'll be working for me."

The youth didn't understand. O'Malley pantomimed in turn. He pointed to the Friar's chest and back to his own, and to his face. "You'll be my eye and ears on that darn boat."

The friar seemed to understand and nodded. "I worka for you."

"As long as those opera singers are in international waters, a captain's arrest would work," O'Malley said. "But I can't send you boys. You don't speak Italian." He thought a few more seconds.

"Get Dominick in here, you know, Dr. Reva's chauffeur. He speaks Italian, and he's in my pocket."

"What about sending Dr. Reva, too?" The rookie asked. "She solved those Aconite murders."

"Do you have to remind me of that?"

Then he snapped his fingers. "You're right! She's got brains, speaks Italian and likes to play amateur detective. She'll solve this case for me."

"Dr. Reva and Dominick are about to get an all expenses paid vacation to Italy," the sergeant laughed. "Like they won the lottery."

"Except there'll be a murderer aboard," the rookie added. "And we'll be sending them into a nest of vipers—fascists."

O'Malley stroked his military style mustache. "Friar Lawrence will report to Dominick. Dominick's a war veteran—he can handle himself. And he's loyal and protective of Dr. Reva.

"They'll be fine—how bad can a few opera-loving fascists be?"

As O'Malley watched the rookie leave with Friar Lawrence, he had a sinking feeling. *If this murder goes unsolved, Brooklyn fascists will make Juliet a martyr for their cause. American fascism could strengthen and divide the citizenry.*

It's looking more and more like war is coming to Europe with the rise of those fascist dictators in Germany, Spain and Italy. If they can get any sympathy for their cause here in the US—this murder could lead to our entry into another war.

If fascism spreads here, there might be more fascist coup attempts against our own government. He thought about the Senate hearings the year before on the fascist-backed Business Plot to overthrow the government and oust President Franklin D. Roosevelt.

"Get me the Commissioner and New York Senator on the horn," he said to his sergeant. "We need to put my plan in action—top priority."

If Dr. Josephine Reva can identify the murdering fascist and thwart a fascist plot, that'd seal another commendation for me. And I'd be preventing an international incident.

"We're gonna need more spies on that boat."

SOLIS MUNDI

Chapter 5 - Josephine's Office

T he late September drizzle washed the city streets of grime and litter, sending murky rivers streaming into the open gutters. The street corners came alive as shop keepers pulled back their wooden shutters and dusted off their shelves. They opened the metal trap doors in the sidewalks to send boxes of goods from the delivery vans flowing into their basement storage.

Dawn was breaking, and if one looked above the low-slung roofs of Brooklyn's three and four-story walk-ups, on a clear day, one could see the spires of Manhattan skyscrapers piercing the clouds. If one looked south, along the sight lines between the buildings created by the broader streets, one could see the Atlantic Ocean beating against Brooklyn's shores.

"Hey, wait up!" Teresa yelled to her siblings, huffing and tussling with her book bag. "Why do we have to go to the doctor so early before school? It's raining, and I'm getting soaked."

"Teresa, stop complainin', you're notta child anymore, you're almost ten years old," her mother, Maria, called over her shoulder, heaving her basket into the arms of her second eldest, eight-year-old Gianni. She put her hands on her hips and yelled, "*Stai attenta!* Be careful, you'll get messy!

"Too late," Teresa sulked, feeling her wet skirt and stockings clumping about her calves. "Why do we always go there every morning? Nobody's sick."

"We're gonna get sick walking there!" wailed the youngest daughter, Chiara, who was four.

"Nobody's not sick," replied Maria in her often double-negated English. "We go to Doc Joe's so I can see all'a my friends, and find out *who did what to who.*"

"It's 'who did what to whom', and you mean the latest gossip," called Antonio, her husband, who was busy in front of his newsstand, hauling huge stacks bundled with cord—the latest editions from around the globe. Because he read the papers every day, his English, in contrast to his wife's, had become fluent. "War news! I'm gonna sell a lot of papers today. Mussolini signed the Stressa Agreement with the British and French."

"Itsa trick," said Maria. "I wouldn't trust that Mussolini. Those thugs, those Blackshirts—"

"Now Maria."

"Mussolini isa dictator. He'sa *pazzo,* crazy. He'sa gonna ruin our country with tat Fascist propaganda."

"Italy could emerge stronger, better, richer."

People in the neighborhood thought Antonio should have been a diplomat—when he wasn't selling newspapers he was reading them. His knowledge of foreign affairs was said to be second only to Roosevelt's.

"Italy, Britain and France signed the pact to oppose Hitler invading his weaker neighbors. That'll keep Italy from getting into trouble."

"What'd Britain and France promise Mussolini? And how soon before Il Duce double-crosses them all?"

"He won't double-cross them. The Stressa Front is a good pact," Antonio contradicted her. "No war. And it's gonna help me sell a lot of papers today!"

"I'm glad you'a follow the front pages—better than reading the sports," huffed Maria. "I dunno how you 'avva so much time for readin', what with all 'a your smokin' and drinkin'."

And gambling, thought Teresa. But she loved her father dearly. He spoiled her and gave her money for *pasticcini,* pastries, at the Italian bakery.

Antonio secretly noted that all hell would break loose if Maria found out about the card games, too.

Maria picked up copies of the Italian paper and the local *Brooklyn Eagle,* folding them into her basket. She would bring these to Doc Joe's.

Antonio continued to stack newspapers. *Every newsstand should carry a wide selection of international opinions.* One day, he'd show his children the great capitals of Europe, and his place of birth, Naples, the best city of them all.

He was born a farmer and belonged to the rich volcanic soils of his native land. But after fifteen years in Brooklyn, he was now part of the cement of this city's life.

Sniffing the briny polluted air, he shrugged. *Che puzza!* W*hatta stink!* The mingling smells of rotting fish, stale bread, muffler exhaust and sweat were hardly appealing. How he missed the Mediterranean scents of rosemary, basil and thyme, those warm turquoise waters he used to dive into from rocky cliffs during his youth. Almost everywhere he went in Naples had views over the clear blue from the houses set in the hillsides. Here, he had to walk over a mile down to The Narrows before he could see the sea, cold and black as ink. *Nope, this was nothing like Naples.*

Yet he felt the beating heart of this metropolis with its exciting new headlines every day.

It's not so bad, he consoled himself. *Business is booming, I've a nice three-story home and all the food we need.* Besides, his children were born here and they were Americans. One day, he and Maria would be naturalized, too. *I'll probably never see Italy again.*

He kissed his wife goodbye as she left for the doctor. He'd find her there later. Going to Doc Joe's was even becoming enjoyable, now that more men were forced to go by their wives. He could catch up on the races with the other fellows.

Maria and her children continued walking until they reached a post-war, industrial one-story brick building, a converted factory. A glass atrium pierced the roofline of the doctor's expansive new office and laboratory. There was a row of parked cars in front, Model A's and Studebakers, but Doc Joe's old luxury Packard was nowhere in sight.

That's swell, thought Maria. *She mustta spent the night with Saltzie after the opera!*

A black metal sign with white lettering hung off the gate stating: "The Doctor is IN". The big square "IN" could be reversed to "OUT", but was rusted in the "IN" position.

"The doctor is always in anyway," remarked Teresa, "'specially now that she's got a new assistant."

The children ran inside, and Maria followed.

"*Dio buono!* Goodness!" exclaimed Maria delightedly, putting down her basket and taking off her scarf. "It's 6 am and dis place is packed!"

"*Che succede*, what's going on?" she asked a woman seated by the door.

"Haven't you heard? It's all over the neighborhood."

Maria's best friend, Sophie, who was the receptionist came running up, and the two greeted each other.

"Why is everyone 'xcited? Do they know about te Stressa Front?"

"The what?"

"What d'ya mean? What'sa happened?" Maria asked Sophie, her good friend and the doctor's receptionist.

Sophie was American born, first generation just like Josephine. She was of English descent, tall and red-haired with green eyes. Her husband, Andy, a Scot, ran the grocers at the corner.

"Mike's pub is open again—it's been more than ten years since they closed it in Prohibition. But Sam's bar and old speakeasy—you know, the one in the basement of his deli—was closed by the health inspector. We're all going out to Mike's tonight to celebrate." Sophie looked at Maria cheerfully.

Maria looked disappointed. "Smokin' and drinkin', that'sa not news." She pulled out her Italian newspaper and pointed to the front page of the international section. "See, Stressa Front. That'sa news. That means no war!"

"That's far away in Europe," sighed Sophie.

But Maria was looking at another article alongside.

"Wowee! I can't believe it," she exclaimed, pointing at the smaller article. The other women gathered around. "Mother Cabrini she'sa venerated."

"That's impossible. It's too quick," a surprised Sophie said.

"Here look!" Maria held up the paper. "The Pope sent dat Cardinal all the way from Roma, bringin' dat special inquisitor."

"You mean Mother Cabrini is now Saint Cabrini?"

"Well, no, not yet. But she'sa step closer—a big step!"

"They're investigating the miracles," another woman chimed in. "Mother Cabrini interceded and cured a blind baby, and the sick, too."

"She's going to be a saint!" Several women chorused and linked arms. "The first *Italian-American* saint."

Maria fell back swooning. "I was'a touched by a Saint!"

Other women began buzzing around her, wanting to hear the story.

One gave her a chair, another fanned her, and then she began to hold court, telling the other ladies about the day Mother Cabrini prayed over her and her children while passing by on a Manhattan street.

Another woman suddenly exclaimed, "Our Doc Joe knew her, too. Wasn't she an orphan in one of Mother Cabrini's homes?"

The group of ladies now buzzed over to this woman, wanting to hear more.

Teresa went to comfort her mother, still collapsed in a chair, and patted her hand. "Don't worry, Mamma, I'll find out all about it."

While Gianni and Chiara stayed with other children, Teresa moved closer to the group of ladies now excitedly whispering.

"Our Doc met Mother Cabrini."

"*Comé lo sai*, how do you know that?"

"We should ask her to tell us the story!"

"But she never talks about her personal life."

"I don't think she would like it if we asked her."

"Let's get Sophie to do it!"

The ladies approached Sophie's desk and asked.

"But I don't know much more than you," Sophie replied. "The subject never came up."

Teresa interjected, "Sometimes people are glad to talk about themselves."

"But not our Doc Joe—she's totally professional. I mean, she has to keep a doctor-patient relationship," Sophie said.

"She don't talk about herself much," Maria came over and said, "even when I'm fitting her for a dress."

"You know, we never tried," Teresa persisted.

"How true," said another woman. "We're always doing the talking."

"Well, the Doc is such a good listener."

There was a chorus of "d*avvero,* true enough," as everyone concurred.

"What can she say about her life, anyway? She's no married and has no children."

"She not even look at a man that way, well, except examining him!"

The women laughed.

"I wonder if she ever made love?" The tittering continued, with peals of laughter.

"Now, ladies, please," Sophie tried to quiet them, to no avail.

"I can't imagine our Doc Joe in the bedroom!"

More raucous laughter exuded from the ladies.

"*Impossibile! La Dottoressa facendo l'amore, non se vede!* The doctor making love, no way!"

The men looked up brightly from their corner, as if on cue.

"Oh, tose men," Maria said. "Every time you talka 'bout sex, their heads pop up!"

"That's how come we have so many children!"

The women giggled, and enjoyed flirtatious glances with their mates.

"Bet ya don't know our Doc Joe was out on a date last night," Maria said. Sophie eyed Maria with a warning look.

The group of ladies now swarmed around Maria, who filled them in on helping Josephine dress for her date with Saltzie.

"With'a my dress, and her hair and make-up done right—once she's outta that lab coat, she's like a little duckling turnin' into a beautiful swan."

The happy party went silent as Josephine's new assistant doctor walked in. A smartly dressed young Irish woman, she wore a tailored plaid suit. She put on her white lab coat, and draped a stethoscope around her neck. Dr. Mabel McGrath spoke to Sophie, then picked up a few charts. In a thick brogue, she called out a few names and led these patients to examination rooms.

Teresa's eyes followed her. *She's beautiful,* thought Teresa, *and a career woman. And she helps people, too. I'm gonna be a doctor like her and Doc Joe one day.*

She noticed Sophie pull the keys from her desk drawer to unlock the atrium. Teresa had never been allowed to enter, and like any child, was curious and followed inside.

Sophie and Maria, with Teresa silently behind, stepped into the atrium to water the plants. Teresa could overhear the adults talking.

"I don't think she'll ever marry," Sophie said. "One date doesn't mean much."

"Ya nevva know," replied Maria.

The plants in the atrium were in bloom, with flowers in hues of pinks, yellows, reds, blues and purples vividly opening towards the sky. The bright petals and green leaves began unfolding to the morning light.

"Isn't the purple Aconite beautiful? It's blooming nicely this year. Look at this cutting - it's taken root," Sophie said.

"Sad tat homeopathic druggist isa dead. But itsa good luck dat Doc Joe could buy tis place cheap atta auction."

"Yes, with five examination rooms, and a new assistant, she can see a lot more patients in a day."

"See tat pink one? I tink itsa very pretty," said Maria.

"Be careful, mamma. That's foxglove. It's deadly." Teresa ran forward to stop her mother from touching it. She then pulled out one of the books in her bag.

"*Digitalis purpurea* is the Latin name. That's the genus and species," she read from her book. "It's deadly but curative, and full of Cardiac glycosides. Digitalis is most commonly used to restore adequate circulation in patients with congestive heart failure, particularly when caused by atherosclerosis or hypertension."

"Very big words, very good, m*olto buono*, Teresa," Sophie said.

"I tink she's gonna be like Doc Joe one day!" Maria said proudly.

"That one with yellow flowers is *Helleborus niger*. I watered it, and the buds are coming out," Sophie showed Teresa a pretty plant with poisonous small white flowers.

"*Helleborus niger*," Teresa consulted her book. "In homeopathy, it relieves nausea, vomiting and diarrhea."

Sophie turned about as green as the leaves. "Let's go back to the waiting room. I need to sit down." She suddenly bent over, and heaved.

"Sophie are you okay?" Maria asked.

"I just feel a little nauseous, that's all."

"Did you touch any plants, or eat any parts of them?" Teresa asked.

"No, of course not."

"That nausea is not from these poison plants," Teresa smiled. "I'd say you're pregnant."

"She's a smart one, that girl," Sophie said. "Teresa, you will make a fine doctor one day."

Maria jumped up and down, hugging Sophie.

"Oh! Sophie, diss wonderful news! You'va waited so long." Maria hugged Sophie. "Now, you'll soon hava your own precious baby! How far along are ya?

"Two months. Doc Joe helped me with treatment for my diabetes, and now—well, she's been a marvel, every step of the way. But don't tell anyone yet," Sophie pleaded.

They returned to the main office waiting room, where the women patients were very excited. The had pulled apart Maria's newspapers and were gathered around the first page of the local news.

"A murder!"

One woman read aloud from the newspaper:

"During last night's performance of the opera Roméo et Juliette, the beautiful young Italian starlet singing the role of Juliet mysteriously died onstage in front of hundreds of spectators.

Even more strange, a young and pretty female doctor happened to be in the audience with her date, another doctor, and they rushed onstage to render aid, but were unable to resuscitate the dying diva.

Brooklyn police seem baffled as to why anyone would kill the young soprano so brutally, or if she committed a horrific suicide by her own hand. Chief Detective John O'Malley said that the public should not be alarmed, and that he would soon have the case solved. But the opera troupe leaves for Italy tomorrow, and whether it's murder or suicide, it looks like the Chief Detective will be out of luck."

"Oh my!" exclaimed several women. "*Che tragedia!* How tragic!"

"It's life imitating art," said another. "In the opera, Juliet dies, and then she dies in real life, too."

Maria eyes grew wide. She found Sophie and whispered. "Isn'ta tat the opera our Doc Joe went to last night?"

"Yes, I was just thinking the same thing. But we'd better keep this between ourselves, okay? It wouldn't help Doc Joe's reputation one bit."

The other ladies were still buzzing about and chatting.

"So who's gonna ask the Doc about Mother Cabrini?" A patient persisted.

"I will!" replied Teresa.

"Out of the mouths of babes—Teresa's the best one to ask."

"But where is Doc Joe?"

"Maybe she's sleeping?"

Peals of incredulous laughter rang out. "Our Doc, sleeping?

"No way!"

"She nevva sleeps!"

The women looked expectantly at the doorway from the waiting room to the hallway. The first opening on the left would be to the galley kitchen. Patients stopped here first to deposit the contents of their baskets into Doc Joe's refrigerator. Home-cooked meals as payment for services. Even with the Great Depression, families like Maria's and Sophie's had a little extra money left after buying food and other necessities. They could cook an extra plate of food for Josephine, who worked around the clock without much time to shop or cook.

The barter system worked fine. As the Depression ebbed, more people were paying in cash again. Josephine still charged $2 for a visit and $3 for a house call, the same as before the Crash. She didn't think it was right to raise rates while so many struggled, and her patients were grateful.

At the end of the long hallway, the ladies remembered, would be the toilets, and more doors leading to examination rooms, five of them, each with a large contraption of a padded leather table with metal stirrup extenders taking up most of the space. Art Deco wood inlaid cabinetry containing metal scalpels, prongs and myriad other medical instruments, a basin and sanitizer, and a doctor's secretary desk. On the shelves they'd see nestled numerous large glass jars with stoppers, filled with wondrous powders and labeled with latinized names like *Antimonium* or *Nux vomica.*

And in a place of prominence, center of the unit, glass ampules filled with new sulfa drugs.

How well they worked—it's miraculous! the ladies thought.

"Is she with someone in an examination room?"

"Nope, I 'avva been 'ere since six o'clock, and nobody 'as come in or outta dose exam rooms."

"Maybe she's in the basement?" Several women paused and thought about that. "Naw, what would she be doing down there?"

"Check if the Packard is in the garage," one man called.

Another ran to look.

"Nope, there's no car in the box," he replied.

"She must be out on a house call."

"Or delivering a baby."

"Sophie didn't say anything about that. We'll just have to wait for our turn with the new assistant."

"Another woman doctor," a man harrumphed. "Irish to boot! I doubt she's any good."

Soon, the proud old 1928 Packard V-8 sedan huffed to a stop at the back of the building.

Dominick, Josephine's chauffeur, still kept his 'baby' washed and gleaming, and its engine roaring. Dominick was of medium tall height and sturdy muscular build, with handsome features and flashing black eyes. His thick shiny black waves were oiled and slicked back. He wore the latest style of suit in pinstripes with red suspenders. He jumped gamely out of the front of the luxury eight-seater, then ran to open one of the rear suicide doors. Out stepped Josephine, still dressed in her evening finery.

The women's jaws dropped. They didn't recognize Josephine at first because of her glamorously flowing silk dress showing off a very shapely body. The neckline was voluptuously low, and she wore a strand of large white pearls.

"Well, I nev'a imagined...," a few voices murmured.

A male patient let out a long wolf whistle.

Josephine turned to wave. At least, her large heart-shaped face with its upturned nose holding up spectacles was the same, but her celestial blue eyes that seemed to fathom all your troubles were now vampishly outlined with a lot of make-up and mascara.

Even her stature was different. On a normal day, she stood barely five foot two inches tall in her doctor's flats, but today she was sporting four-inch heels and looked almost statuesque. Her thick black hair was no longer in a tight bun, with several pins gone, and several messy strands flowed loosely about her shoulders, giving her a care-free look.

As she turned to grab her medical bag from the back seat, the naked back of her dress, and the seam in the skirt torn to her thigh, revealed far more than she imagined. Her patients gasped.

My, my!" cooed one patient, "look who's been putting on the Ritz!"

"She must've been out with that doctor fella, the one who's a bootlegger," said another.

"Dr. Saltzman. They were out for a dinner and a show," said Sophie, trying to impart an air of respectability.

"She must've stayed out all night with him," said a patient, "she hasn't even changed her clothes."

"Saltzman? Ya mean the doc who's a jailbird?"

"I heard the two of them are now as thick as thieves," another said. "Although Doc of course, isn't a thief. It's just an expression."

"He didn't serve any time in the Big House, so he's not a jailbird. He's a respectable gastroenterologist," Sophie said.

"Word is he got off on a technicality."

"He's now one of the best doctors in Manhattan, with celebrity patients," Sophie said.

"Go figure."

Sophie sighed, as patients began whispering. There'd be no stopping the gossip mill.

"I wonder what they were up to all night long?" a patient asked.

"You know what they were up to! And it's about time. Good for our Doc," another answered.

"She needs to marry him soon—she's not getting any younger."

"They could have baby doctors."

"She's almost in her mid-thirties, and he's even older, almost forty."

"Goodness, that's old!"

"Yes, let's say a prayer to Mother Cabrini. Lord knows our Doc needs a push."

"A shove, more likely."

Josephine, meanwhile, was making her way to the back entrance, throwing her fur stole over her shoulders, and stopping to adjust the strap on the back of her high-heeled evening shoes, which were killing her.

These heels are so bad for my metacarpals, talus and navicular. She continued limping along painfully.

She turned to look behind her and beckoned. Dominick was gingerly carrying her black leather bag containing all the tools of her trade.

They hurriedly went to the back entry to avert more curious patient gazes.

"Dominick, thank you for picking me up at the police station. But remember, we've got to keep my involvement in this murder zipped for now," Josephine whispered. "I don't want to alarm my patients. We don't know if there are other murderous, opera-singing fascists on the loose in Brooklyn. Let them think I spent the night at Saltzie's."

"OK, anything you say, Doc. But I've got a feeling that the dames are already spreading the lie about you and Saltzie doing the *whatoozie*. You know how the Brooklyn grapevine works." He nodded towards the patients giggling.

"As long as they're not gossiping about my involvement in any murder. I'll have to sort it out later." They had reached the main floor and walked down the hallway to Josephine's office, avoiding the waiting room with its closed door, and continued to whisper.

"I know you don't like Saltzie, but I believe that criminals can reform. Besides, he's no murderer." She took off her stole and hung it up in the coat closet. She peeled off her long white evening gloves, flecked with blood and vomit. She went into the bathroom, closing the door, and started to undress.

"Please hand me my plaid housedress, the blue one, please?"

Dominick averted his gaze as he passed her the housedress, but couldn't resist taking a peek through the crack in the door. Josephine passed him her evening attire.

"It's not that I don't like Saltzie," Dominick said, fingering her silks, then hanging them in the armoire. "But I know what criminals are like, and I don't trust him—."

"Whom I don't trust now is the killer. We need to find out what those fascist opera stars were doing in Brooklyn. I think there's more to this story."

"You mean, why was that diva singing about Mussolini?"

"Yes, exactly. I need to find out what she was up to."

"She was a fascist, that's what. She was beautiful, but she was a disgusting pig like the rest of 'em."

"She was singing to someone in the audience. I'm sure of it. She used "*Lei*" as if she was addressing someone respectable."

"Mussolini, more than likely."

"I don't know, but she wasn't working alone." Josephine emerged from the bathroom in her housedress.Then she stepped out of her evening shoes and sat down to affix her flat doctor's shoes. "Why was any of that troupe even here? I don't think it was a cultural exchange between La Scala and Brooklyn."

"You think her singing was intended to send a message to someone in Brooklyn?"

"Yes, I do. Wasn't the performance broadcast on the local radio, too?"

"Yes, it was. I listened to it on my radio."

"Oh dear, then she could have been singing to anyone in the entire city!" Josephine stood up.

"Well, let's take another tactic," Dominick said as he helped her into her white lab coat, lightly touching Josephine's shoulders. "She was poisoned. What does that tell us?"

"The poison worked in less than thirty minutes, and brought on hallucinations. I think it was Belladonna—eating a handful of berries would be lethal."

"Does that bring on hallucinations?"

"Yes. I need a sample of the poison from that bottle—then I could test it and know for sure."

"I'll go back and look for it."

"No, Detective O'Malley warned me to stay away from the crime scene. It's just speculation for now."

"Doc, maybe you'd better check your atrium and see if any poisonous plants are missing from the lab."

"Oh, dear, I hope someone isn't trying to implicate me again, like the Aconite murders," Josephine sighed. "You're right, I'd better check. It's already seven o'clock in the morning—I'm late. Time to face my patients. How do I look?"

Beautiful, Dominick thought to himself, and gave her a thumbs up.

Josephine entered her office area, and found Sophie at the desk. Sophie was wearing a loose-fitting green dress with wide white lapels.

"Sophie, you look so lovely today," she whispered. "Being pregnant is certainly making you glow."

"Never mind me," Sophie said with a wink. "You're glowing, too."

"Thank you very much."

"That's *Tante grazie.* I'm learning Italian. Andy has promised to take me and the baby to Rome, well, one day."

"You'll be so busy with the new baby. But I'm sure Italian will come in useful here in Brooklyn. You can always speak to my Italian patients like Maria."

Sophie started to look a little green again.

"It's completely normal that you'd feel a little indigestion and nausea. Here, I'll make you some of my ginger tea. Ginger helps with nausea."

"I'm fine, really, Doc," Sophie replied. "I'm so excited to have a baby. I don't mind the discomfort one bit." She grabbed the edge of her desk.

"I think you should lie down and rest in back. And you shouldn't tend the poison plants any longer. Dominick will do it."

"No, I feel fine. And I'll be careful. I love looking at the flowers and thinking how deadly they are. I'll never water them unless I wear gloves."

"Still let's have Dominick, or the new assistant, do the watering from now on. I'm concerned for your safety. But you can tend the non-poisonous flowers where the patients wait."

"Okay," Sophie sighed. "Speaking of danger, Maria and I read the morning paper." She handed the edition to Josephine.

"That Brooklyn grapevine is fast!" Josephine frowned.

"What exactly happened?"

"I can't say yet, and I don't want to alarm you or my patients. But it looks like the diva was murdered."

"This city is crime-ridden."

"I mean, it was probably one of the other opera stars or someone she knew," Josephine explained. "Please don't spill the beans to anyone yet. But importantly, please tell me you saw all the poison plants today in the atrium?"

"I'm not sure. I was feeling queasy."

"Oh dear!"

"Do you mean to say that you suspect there's been another poison plant murder?" Sophie exclaimed.

"Shhh! Sophie, please keep this quiet."

Josephine took the atrium key.

"I'd better go check."

They walked into the atrium together, and Sophie picked up a watering can. Josephine shook her head to stop her.

"But the article said that it could be suicide," Sophie said.

"I'm sure it was murder." Josephine paused. "Her illness happened after Friar Lawrence gave her the poison to take to feign death."

"Just like in Shakespeare's Romeo and Juliet!"

"Yes, well, no. It was Gounod's musical version of the play."

"I'll call my husband. Andy knows Shakespeare by heart, although he prefers Macbeth—he's Scottish. you know. "

Josephine agreed, although she didn't see what that had to do with it.

Sophie went back to the office telephone desk to place the call as Maria and Teresa came into the atrium.

"How was your night at the opera? Romeo and Juliet is so romantic. Did Saltzie kiss you?"

"Aren't you going to ask me about the death onstage?"

"Nope, who cares? I wanna know if Dr. Saltzman proposed."

"Actually Saltzie proposed several times, sort of."

"But you'va got no ring." Maria was disappointed as she examined Josephine's hand.

Sophie re-entered the atrium.

"Guess what poison Juliet took in the play—Belladonna."

"Well, yes, I read the libretto," Josephine said. "The scientific name is *Atropa belladonna*."

"Maybe the murderer wanted to follow the play exactly?"

"But in the play, Juliet killed herself with a dagger."

Teresa, who had been listening intently to the ladies, silently searched for *Atropa belladonna* in the pocket plant book. "It says here that the juice of the berries is full of Atropine and Hyosamine. I think the murderer could have crushed the berries and given Juliet the juice to drink."

Maria turned to her daughter. "Teresa! You'da better not be turning into a detective."

"No, Mamma. I'm interested purely from a medical perspective."

"Oh, *Dio Buono*, Goodness! My daughter take'a after you, Doc Joe."

"Let's find the Belladonna plant," said Josephine. "I want to make sure it's still here."

They searched until they saw it in its ceramic pot, under the apex of the atrium's pyramidal roof. The plant was waking up to the morning light, stretching its bright green leaves outward. The small purple flowers extended from the stems, adding a nice color, but it was the many indigo black berries set like cabochons in the middle of five-petal leaf bursts that gave the plant its beauty.

Josephine reached to touch it, but stopped herself. *It's enticing, but deadly. Did it kill Juliet and why?*

"Let's go back to the office," she breathed a sigh of relief. "I'd better start seeing my patients."

The ladies and Teresa exited the atrium, with Sophie locking the door.

Sophie pulled out the calendar. "You have several house calls today. I don't know how you're going to see all these patients in the waiting room, plus your house calls.

"I have my new assistant. She can take the house calls today."

"Teresa can help," said Maria. "She follows you around like'a little shadow. She'sa very smart and remembers everyting, and she's good with her hands. She crochets and sews all 'a the time. Look, she made you dis lace doily to sit under the telephone so you don'ta scratch the table." She placed the doily under the ringer box.

"Thank you," Josephine said.

Looking at the crowd in Josephine's waiting room, Sophie decided the matter.

"Teresa, you can help me today by taking a file from this pile, calling out the name, then greeting and weighing the patient. Ask them to remove their shoes and step on the scale. You adjust these counterweights. The big one is the hundreds, the middle is tens, then you slide this marker for the ones. See? Can you add it all up?" Teresa nodded. "Good, then you note the weight next to the date here. Lastly, you can lead the patient to an empty examination room."

"Do I get to wear a white lab coat?" Teresa asked.

"Not yet, but one day, if you study."

Teresa trotted happily off, following Sophie to the waiting room.

Maria led the way to Josephine's office.

"Did'a Saltzie give you these?" She fingered the huge pearls sitting on the desk. "They're as big as'a eggs!"

"Yes, he did, but I'm going to return them."

"Why? I betcha dey worth a fortune."

"Accepting a gift like that from a man would give him certain expectations."

"And would tat be a bad ting?"

Josephine harrumphed. "I'm not getting married. I've a busy practice. I wouldn't have time to be a wife. Now I'd best get back to it."

Maria just smiled and stepped aside, as Josephine headed toward an examination room.

Chief Detective O'Malley was sitting on the examination table, examining the stirrups with a queer expression. He stood up in embarrassment when Josephine walked in. She knew he was tall, but in her small examination room, he filled it like an oak tree.

"Detective, you startled me! You look queasy. Are you unwell?"

She took his pulse. "Haven't you taken those vitamins I prescribed for you? Vitamin A and C, and especially the B vitamins should help with your energy levels. The most important thing is to get enough sleep, which I don't think you've been doing."

"I'm not here about my health, Dr. Reva. I've a small, er, favor to ask of you."

"A favor? From me? Oh, you really are unwell. I'd best take a look at you. Please unbutton your shirt."

The detective struggled to remove his tie and shirt. Josephine prodded his naked torso. She noticed that his chest was broad, his pectorals solid, and his bicep and tricep muscles bulged. "No sign of tuberculosis."

His body did look in peak condition. "No sign of any concavity of the chest," she added.

"You heard the diva singing about Mussolini," he began, but Josephine stuck a thermometer in his mouth. After she noted his temperature, he continued. "It seems some members of the opera troupe were making contact with Brooklyn fascists."

"What's that got to do with me?" She wrapped a blood pressure band around his arm and began pumping up the pressure. "Surely, you don't think that I know anything about that. Are you accusing me of a crime again?"

"No, Doctor—hey, don't get mad. Go easy with that pump—I feel like my arm's about to break off."

"Relax, please. I have to pump it up to see if you're hypertensive. Please try to stay still."

"I hate these newfangled medical things. Next you'll be opening me up and sticking pins in me."

Josephine smiled as she released the pressure and unwrapped the band from his arm. She made some notes in his chart.

"Now, what were you saying about fascists?" She placed her stethoscope over his heart, then moved it across his chest, careful not to entangle her fingers in his thick hair.

"I believe you're right. Juliet's death was a murder. And it has to do with a Brooklyn Fascist group joining Italian Fascists."

"Breathe deeply," said Josephine, moving her stethoscope to his back. "Now cough." The detective complied with all her requests, which she found odd.

"You're healthy and strong." She put down her stethoscope and looked at him expectantly. "Why are you here?"

The detective blurted it out. "I'd like you to sail tomorrow for Naples with the opera troupe, find the murderer and make a citizen's arrest."

Josephine laughed. "Detective, are you having another of your migraines? Your judgement has completely left you."

She pulled out her prescription pad and looked at him sadly.

"I'm going to increase your Belladonna prescription. Increasing means a lower number, remember. The Law of Infinitesimals: the more dilute, the more powerful. And I recommend *Coffea*, to help you relax from all that coffee you drink. Caffeine is a stimulant." She started writing. "We'll see if we can get your mind working properly again."

"My mind is working fine. I'm telling you that this is urgent. We have an opportunity to catch the head of this fascist snake-like organization and cut it off—before the boat reaches Naples."

"Snakes? Are you serious?"

"Yes, I am. I've spoken to our Senator. This group has infiltrated several high ranking business groups—wealthy individuals with fascist leanings. There were Senate hearings only last year, and according to witness testimony, they conspired to launch a coup against the President."

"FDR! Who'd want to assassinate him?" Josephine stuck a tongue depressor in the detective's mouth and asked him to say "ahh".

"Uh huh," the detective nodded. Josephine said that he didn't have any fever or sign of a sore throat.

"You just need some sleep. Please put your shirt back on." She snuck a peek from behind her chart as he dressed.

O'Malley buttoned up his shirt and knotted his tie. "Fascist Blackshirts use violence to control people. They're murderous thugs who kill their opponents. They'll stop at nothing to take down our democracy, and aim to spread their poison across the world."

"Juliet did sing about Mussolini wanting to invade Abyssinia."

"If he succeeds, and then joins up with Hitler, that could force us into another world war—one we might lose."

"You think that whoever killed Juliet is the head of this organization?"

"We think she was working for him."

"Why would they kill one of their own?"

"We don't know. That's why we need your help. All you have to do is take a luxury cruise to Italy and question all the opera stars. Find out what they're up to."

"Luxury cruise? Me? Alone?"

"I'm sending Dominick with you. He'll keep you out of harm's way."

Josephine couldn't help imagining herself sunning on an ocean liner deck chair, then seeing the sites of Italy, along with any medical laboratories she could find. "First Class?"

The detective harrumphed. "All right, First Class, it is. You'll be among the opera stars then."

"But how am I going to question all of them on an ocean liner, and find the murderer in a few days, all by myself?"

"Well, you could take that beau of yours to help."

"He doesn't speak any Italian." Josephine would be glad for an opportunity to escape Saltzie's romantic clutches. She still wasn't sure she wanted to marry at all.

"What about those Italian friends of yours? The ones who helped you on the Aconite cases?"

"Maria and Antonio. What a good idea, Detective." Josephine smiled.

"I'll arrange their tickets. What you're about to do is important for the country."

Josephine paused. *A first class trip to Naples, for free.* She could finally scatter her mother's ashes in the bay, her final wish. All she had to do was question Mussolini's opera singers. *What could possibly go wrong?*

"Will we be safe?"

"Yes, besides Dominick, the Feds are sending someone from their team. The Fascists won't harm any Americans—they want Americans to convert to Fascism and support Mussolini."

He pulled on his jacket and fedora.

"You'll pretend to be opera singers from an amateur Brooklyn group heading to Italy on vacation. I've heard you sing, you'll do fine. Mingle with those fascist divas and dons. With any luck, they'll try to convince you to join their cause. Then all you have to do is meet their leader."

Chapter 6 - Aboard the S.S. Rex

Come, bitter conduct, come, unsavory guide!
Thou desperate pilot, now at once run on
The dashing rocks thy sea-sick weary bark!
  —Romeo and Juliet by William Shakespeare

C onfetti streamers flew in the air like the colorful wings of butterflies, as Josephine, Dominick, Maria and Antonio leaned over the deck rails, waving goodbye to the crowds.

"Isn't this exciting!" Josephine said to her burly chauffeur standing next to her.

Dominick was seeking to impress her by reading from the *SS Rex* brochure.

"They call her 'the greyhound of the seas.' The *SS Rex* was built for speed. She's 50,000 tonnes, 880 feet long by almost 100 feet wide. She's the first Mediterranean-style resort ship—there's real sand and beach umbrellas around the pool! Wow, there's even a pool!" He pointed to several beautiful illustrations in the brochure.

"She first sailed from Genoa in September 1932, after a send-off from Premier Benito Mussolini himself. There were a ton of celebrities aboard."

"I don't care at all about those celebrities," said Josephine. "Nor about any luxury. How long does this voyage take?"

"Okay, Doc. It says on her maiden voyage, the ship had serious mechanical issues off the coast of Gibraltar. Repairs took three extra days." He reflected for an instant, then continued.

"Half of the passengers got off and took a train all the way to Germany to catch the *Europa*. But when they arrived in New York, they were surprised to find the *SS Rex* already at the dock!"

He skipped over some details about the ship's engine. "The *SS Rex* returned to Genoa on October 26, 1932, making her first eastbound crossing in only six and a half days. Soon, she won the Blue Riband in August of 1933, heading westbound with a time of only four days and thirteen hours, with an average speed of 28.92 knots. That's 53.56 km/h; or 33.28 mph— she's as fast as our Packard." He laughed, then continued.

"This record lasted until June of this year, 1935, when the French *Normandie* won. It says here that our Captain will try to break another record on this crossing."

"Oh dear! I hope he doesn't. Goodness, only 6 ½ days! How am I going to solve this case and make an arrest in less than a week?"

Dominick studied the brochure's diagram of the ship's engines and propellers. "Don't worry. You'll have plenty of time to catch the killer. I'll see to that."

The dual smokestacks of the *SS Rex* shot plumes of black smoke into the Manhattan sky, and its horn blasted a stern warning. She was ready to depart.

Deckhands were throwing huge twisted ropes from the pier back onto the foredeck and stern, and several others pulled up the gangway.

The massive ship was now free from the dock.

The *SS Rex* sounded her horn again. One prolonged blast and three short ones to signal it was underway and shifting gears into reverse. The grand ship began edging into the Hudson River.

"Goodbye, New York! Goodbye, America!" shouted Josephine. She threw streamers and waved excitedly to her patients on the dock below.

As the sun set, the great bulk of a ship began ploughing through the Hudson River. The pilot tug boat guided her through the currents, expertly avoiding the many cargo ships and ferry traffic.

Soon, the crowds were just specks on the horizon, and Josephine stopped waving.

With another plume of black smoke, the *SS Rex* made its way downstream. Josephine could see the tall spire of the Woolworth Building and the Battery shipyards.

The *SS Rex* passed from the Hudson River into the great mouth of New York Bay, heading towards Governor's Island.

On the *Ponte passagiato*, or Promenade Deck, many passengers dabbed at their eyes with handkerchiefs, having left their loved ones in America behind. Some had failed in their hopes of finding a better life, but some had succeeded and were taking their tales and earnings back to Italy. "*Arriverderci! We'll see you again one day,*" they cried.

Josephine could see Lady Liberty up ahead. Soon the ship would slip into The Narrows, that wine press of a channel funneling Atlantic waters between Staten Island and Brooklyn.

"Look, I think I see our brick house," Maria asked, pointing to Brooklyn to the east.

"Of course you can," replied her husband indulgently. "I can see the Clock Tower at the end of the Brooklyn Bridge."

"We'll soon make our way through The Narrows, then it's through the Bight, then the Ambrose Channel and out into open water," Dominick announced excitedly.

Josephine and her friends leaned on the rail, not wanting to let Brooklyn fade away. She remembered the Aconite murder at The Narrows five years before, when she'd examined the body at the scene of the crime. Josephine had a sense of foreboding, and shivered.

Out of nowhere, Saltzie appeared by her side, covered in confetti, and holding two fizzy champagne glasses. He handed one to Josephine with a wink.

"SURPRISE!"

"I'm shocked—" Josephine stammered.

"What she means is, she'sa delighted!" said Maria, practically throwing Josephine into Saltzie's arms.

"Steady on, now!" he said, happily grabbing Josephine around the waist as the ship rocked. "You must've known that you couldn't keep me away for long!"

Josephine had to admit that she was really pleased to see Saltzie again since their date at the opera hadn't ended as planned. She took in his profile once more—a strong straight nose, intelligent high forehead, dazzling deep brown eyes. But that rakish smile, she knew all too well. He'd always be a *Yorkvillain* to her, although an awfully handsome one.

He was dashingly dressed, in a light summer linen suit and even sporting a yachtsman's cap. She was surprised to feel her heart skip a beat, whether it was Maria's push, his arms around her, or the gently rocking ship with gusts of sea air whipping off the waves. The voyage no longer seemed dangerous, but romantic.

She nudged herself a bit closer to him while gripping the railing.

"Saltzie! How'd you get a ticket? If you don't have one, they'll arrest you as a stowaway."

"Joe, I couldn't let you go off to dangerous fascist Italy without me." Saltzie held up a First Class ticket.

Spotting Dominick, he frowned. "I didn't know you were bringing your 'fire extinguisher' along."

"No need to worry, buddy," Dominick was flexing his biceps. "I'm able to protect Doc Josephine without you."

He pointed to the ship's brochure. "There's a gym aboard. Why don't we plan on some wrestling?"

"Wrestling? How ungentlemanly. I challenge you to a bout of fencing. I hear there'll be a tournament." He frowned as Dominick flexed his thick muscles again. "Oh, too bad, it's for First Class passengers only."

"I'm in First Class, too," said Dominick, holding up his own ticket. "How hard can fighting with swords instead of sticks be?" He slapped Saltzie hard on the back. "See you at the tournament."

Saltzie sputtered but recovered quickly. "Sorry you'll miss out on all the fun—I could only carry two coupes." He handed Josephine one of the champagne coupes.

He raised the coupe to his lips, and looked into Josephine's eyes. *It'll all be worth it*, he thought. Never one to let a rather large obstacle such as Dominick stand in his way, he toasted his gal with a flirty wink and a smile. They entwined their arms like a pair of swans' necks.

Together they took another sip of champagne, their noses and lips almost touching.

Dominick slapped Saltzie on the back again. He grabbed a coupe from a passing waiter and raised his glass.

"*Buon viaggio!* To a safe voyage!"

"*Speriamo*, I certainly hope so," sighed Josephine.

"Don't worry, I'm here now." Saltzie took Josephine in his arms, while warily eyeing Dominick.

"Saltzie, please," whispered Josephine. "Remember, I need Dominick's help."

"Let's drink to a marvelous new adventure," she said aloud, smiling at Dominick.

"And let's hope it doesn't end up with Saltzie in jail again. Right, buddy?"

"Remember I saved her last time, buddy," protested Saltzie.

Josephine put her hand up to the men. "Now boys. Please stop fighting. We're on a mission, remember? All we have to do is mingle with the passengers, and find out who's their fascist leader."

"Is that all?" Saltzie sputtered. "Is that what Detective O'Malley wants to use you for—"

"*Buon viaggio!* My friends, here's to a wonderful voyage," toasted Antonio, attempting to silence Saltzie in case any suspects were nearby. "And here's to seeing Naples once more with my beautiful bride, *brindiamo alla mia bellissima sposa*." He toasted Maria and she giggled, raising her glass.

"Indeed, *le belle spose*," said Saltzie, toasting Maria and winking at Josephine. "I've been practicing Italian for the trip."

Saltzie tilted his champagne coupe in Josephine's direction.

All five clinked glasses.

Maria and Antonio linked arms and went for stroll around the deck.

As the sky turned purple and the stars began to shine, the ship steered towards the rocky Ambrose Channel. It steamed past Coney Island, and Saltzie excitedly pointed out the giant ferris wheel and Cyclone rollercoaster.

"Look, Josephine! Take my binoculars. There's my house and dock at Seagate—you can just make it out over by the point." He guided her to look. "There in the distance, by the Coney Island lighthouse." Saltzie pointed to a spit of sandy beach.

"I remember the night we spent there, six years ago." She gave him a smile. Saltzie put his arm around Josephine and drew her closer.

"Remember that beacon?" he asked, as he snuggled against her cheek. "It was magical."

"It didn't have anything to do with magic, "she replied matter-of-factly. "Bootlegging was more like it."

"Remember the kitchen where we got cozy over some Long Island oysters?" he continued undeterred.

"Not really," she lied, "but I remember that emetic bowl."

"Remember the bedroom where we snuggled like two bugs in a rug?"

"I remember that armored speedboat coming to your dock and interrupting us."

"And I remember the police coming to haul you and your bootlegging friends off to jail," Dominick added.

"Let's not bring up old memories," shrugged Saltzie. "It's time for new ones. *Romantica Italia arriviamo*—onward to romantic Italy!"

He smiled. "Now, I'll tell you my news. Good and bad. Which do you want to hear first, Josephine?"

"Tell me the good first."

"I've booked a huge suite on board."

"And that's the good news?" Dominick muttered.

"What about your bad news?" Josephine asked.

Saltzie turned his body to Josephine, opening his arms. "You're the doctor—examine me."

"What do you mean? Are you ill?"

"No, Josephine, don't be concerned. I didn't mean to frighten you."

Just then, an elegantly dressed woman interrupted them. She was wearing a bright turquoise silk traveling suit covering her portly frame, a large sun hat with a yellow bow far larger than anything Josephine had ever seen, and huge white framed sunglasses. But in an instant, Josephine recognized the woman.

"Mrs. Porter-Graves! What a coincidence! Are you heading to Nice, Genoa or Naples?"

"Naples. Dr. Reva, it's a pleasure to find you again. Please call me Henrietta, if I may call you Josephine, as we're bosom buddies."

Josephine smiled and nodded.

Henrietta noted the intimacy between Josephine and Saltzie. "And who's this handsome devil, your fiancé?"

"Dr. Charles Saltzman, pleased to make your acquaintance. You must be Mrs. Porter-Graves. I've seen your picture in the society pages."

He whispered to Josephine, "I usually make the A list myself."

But Josephine looked confused. "A or B? What's the difference?"

"Not one but two handsome suitors," Henrietta said indicating Dominick. "You are fortunate indeed Josephine." She smiled charmingly at the men, proving she had once been a fair catch herself.

94

"And you all may call me Henrietta. Any friend of Josephine's is a friend of mine."

Saltzie signaled to a waiter to bring another champagne coupe.

"I read the early edition of the *Brooklyn Eagle*," continued Henrietta, "about the suspicious death of the Italian soprano. Imagine that! It happened right onstage at the Brooklyn Opera House —how shocking! The article also mentioned that there was a pretty woman doctor in the audience who rushed to render aid. How many woman doctors are there in Brooklyn? Then I heard that you, Josephine, had joined an opera troupe."

Mrs. Porter-Graves lowered her voice. "I said to myself, now there has to be something more to this story. A successful doctor ups and leaves her practice to join the opera? Hardly likely." She laughed so strongly that the large pearls on her chest bounced like foam bubbles floating on the sea. "Perhaps Dr. Reva is once again unravelling another mystery?"

"Please," Josephine implored, "you mustn't say anything to the other passengers."

"My lips are sealed. I only told my daughter, and she loves a good mystery, too. So we decided to book our passage to come and watch you in action. Besides, it's time to visit Italy again, before the war starts and we won't be able to travel to Europe at all."

She announced to the group, "You must all come stay with us at our villa in Capri. There's plenty of room." She lowered her voice to Josephine. "After you've solved the mystery you can tell us all about it, of course."

"Your daughter is with you?"

"Yes, she's talking with the famous Signora Schiavone and Signore Delitto over there." Josephine shrugged her shoulders.

"You've not heard of those two? She's an outrageous fashion designer and he's a crazy artist. Very entertaining." She admonished Josephine. "It's time you started attending to society women as a personal physician. It will greatly increase your income." She eyed Josephine's simple traveling suit.

"I'm perfectly fine doing what I'm doing."

"Olivia! Where is that daughter of mine!" Henrietta's voice boomed across the deck. She turned back to Josephine. "After your speech at our Ladies' Luncheon in 1929, when you encouraged more women to enter medicine—well, Olivia just passed her exams!'

"That's wonderful news!"

"Here she comes now."

They turned to look. A lovely tall woman turned away from the artists to walk over. She was stunning with blonde curly hair, and seemed to beam as bright as any lighthouse. She walked with an obvious limp and used a silver-topped cane, which made her all the more distinctive. Josephine could tell that one of her legs was shorter than the other, despite some shoe heel prosthetics, but that did nothing to detract from her charisma. Olivia wore a gorgeous sailor suit linen dress in white and navy, and a beautiful hat with a real ostrich feather that seemed to billow like a cloud from the ship's smokestack.

"May I present my daughter, Olivia. Or I should say *Doctor* Olivia Porter-Graves."

Olivia was portly, too, measuring equally to her mother's operatic form, and her height being equal to a man's.

Olivia beamed. She greeted everyone, but her eyes lingered over Dominick, with his dashing dark looks and flashing black eyes.

She smiled at him, extending her hand for an extra moment. "Pleased to meet you, *Piacere di conoscerelo.*"

"Your Italian is very good," said Dominick, and he took her hand in his and kissed it. "*Molto piacere*, I'm honored."

He took in her buxom form with an overt once over, and smiled broadly, holding her gaze.

Olivia batted her green eyes at Dominick and the two exchanged more than a look.

"Med school must have been hard—did they tease you, the boys, I mean, for being a girl?" Saltzie asked. "We *Yorkvillains* were very naughty to Josephine. One time we locked her in the morgue for an entire night."

"No man could ever keep me from doing what I was meant to do." Olivia nodded sympathetically to Josephine.

"A modern woman who follows her heart as well as her own mind," Dominick said. Olivia gave him a wink.

Her mother looked alarmed. "Now Olivia, you really mustn't get excited." She turned to the group. "Ever since she was a child, she's been so adventurous. I'm so protective of her, because of, well, her deformity."

"Oh, mother, stop! I'm perfectly capable."

"From where I'm standing, I only see perfection and beauty, *la bellezza*," said Dominick, staring into Olivia's lovely eyes.

Olivia giggled. "And I see *un'uomo bello*, a handsome man."

Dominick's chest puffed out like a peacock.

"More champagne for everyone!" Saltzie laughed and signaled for a waiter. He was immensely pleased that Dominick had his eye on another fish in the sea. The less competition he had for Josephine's attention on this cruise the better, for he had decided that he was going to propose to her. He hid a very impressive two-carat diamond ring, with the diamond flanked by two Ceylon sapphires, in his breast pocket.

He just needed the right romantic moment to pop the question.

How hard could that be on a romantic cruise to the Mediterranean aboard a luxury ocean liner?

He knew that Josephine was a practical girl, the kind that giving a toaster to was appreciated, but still he suspected she was a romantic at heart.

A waiter brought more champagne coupes for the Porter-Graves, and the group toasted to a memorable Atlantic crossing.

As they drank, Cardinal Schlummer and the Devil's Advocate solemnly walked by in black cassocks and purple Papal regalia. The Devil's Advocate led in front, carrying an enormous ornate gilt bronze crucifix, and the cardinal followed carrying a polished wooden and brass box.

"Who are they," Henrietta asked Josephine.

"Papal emissaries, and those are the relics of Mother Cabrini in that box. She'll soon be our first American saint."

The passengers stopped to watch the procession.

The cardinal nodded to Josephine. The Devil's Advocate took a good look at the group holding their champagne coupes and frowned.

"He doesn't look like he's ever had any fun," remarked Olivia.

"Yes, he's so serious," said Josephine. "But they are on a sacred mission."

The cardinal and Devil's Advocate headed into the ship's main lobby. The procession stopped and started, as many passengers tried to touch or kiss the box.

"Well, it's getting dark," said Mrs. Porter-Graves. "Come Olivia, we must go find our stateroom and rest before dinner. I don't want you to tire yourself. Will you excuse us?"

"Of course, my ladies." Dominick reluctantly let go of Olivia's hand. "And I must head up to the bridge. I've urgent business with the captain."

Olivia looked impressed. "Will I see you at dinner?" she gave him a seductive smile. Dominick noticed that her ample form jiggled as the boat rocked.

"Olivia, don't be ridiculous. We've an invitation to dine at the captain's table." Her mother grabbed her arm.

"Steady," Dominick grabbed her other arm as she stumbled while turning with her cane. His blood was pounding.

The Porter-Graves walked off, Olivia slowly with her cane while pushing her mother's arm away.

The southern coast of Brooklyn and Long Island became no more than a spark of twinkling lights in the distance. The open waters ahead seemed calm enough, thought Josephine, whose nautical experience only extended to day trips on the Staten Island Ferry. Nonetheless, she felt the boat begin to rock.

Saltzie put his arm around Josephine's waist as the boat sliced through the heavier seas. He drew her closer. "Now for my bad news."

She was concerned and pressed against him, but feeling something hard, she moved back in alarm. "Wow, what's that?"

"Something for you."

Josephine moved closer again against his hardness.

"Is that a pistol in your pocket, or are you happy to see me?" She was feeling giddy from the champagne and mimicked Mae West's sexy voice. Maybe it was the rough rocking of the ship on the waves, or the excitement of the voyage that led to this momentary lapse of her normally reserved nature.

"Wow, I never heard you speak like that, Joe!" Saltzie drew Josephine closer.

"I overheard my patients repeating that line after they saw the movie."

She brought her hand down towards his pants pocket.

"Don't push too hard—you'll break it."

"What?"

"It's not my anatomy," he whispered in her ear, his breath tingling her senses.

She felt the outline of an oval form and she knew. "It's the missing poison bottle!"

"Yes."

"How'd you get it?"

"That's the bad part. I had to commit a crime. I followed Friar Lawrence to a back alley behind the opera house, and then I thumped him and snatched it from his pocket."

"Good thinking!"

"Let's go back to my cabin and you can pull it out of my pants."

"I can't wait!"

She grabbed his hand and turned towards the grand staircase leading to First Class.

"Nice when a woman is so eager." Saltzie gave Dominick a smirk over his shoulder as he hurried off, trailing Josephine.

But Dominick's thoughts were elsewhere as he headed towards the Bridge, a bit lighter in his step from his encounter with the voluptuous Dr. Olivia Porter-Graves.

Chapter 7 - The Bridge

A s Dominick climbed the metal stairs leading to the Bridge, he noticed a speedboat racing to meet the ship. *Who's arriving so late? That's some VIP.*

The *SS Rex* ground to a crawl, its gears wrenched into reverse. "Steady! Come alongside," a deckhand called as he threw a heavy rope to the speedboat. A door in the massive hull opened and a rope ladder was dropped into the speedboat. A man dressed in a white tie evening dinner jacket latched onto the rope ladder and began climbing.

Dominick watched wonderingly. He asked a group of deckhands about the VIP.

"Sta arrivando il capitano. The captain is coming aboard."

"He's like a cat, our Capitano Bevilacqua, out all night, prowling and putting on the Ritz. It's the same in every port of call."

"He likes to make a grand entrance, that one," added another sailor.

Inside could be heard cries of "Prepare the Bridge!" as Dominick entered. A good-looking officer was standing at the ship's wheel, idling the ship's powerful engines to keep her steady.

"Capitano Bevilacqua, fashionably late as usual. He's just in the nick of time before we're fully out of the Ambrose and into the Atlantic. Then he'd have to parachute aboard."

The 'all clear' order was given.

The officer scowled and set the lever back to forward. The massive ship gave a lurch and slowly took on speed.

"This is going to throw off my timed run to Gibraltar. How am I going to break the speed record and retake my Blue Riband?"

"Yours?" Dominick asked. "You mean the Captain's, don't you?"

"No, I mean my Blue Riband." The officer turned to look at Dominick, glancing up and down at him, noticing his muscular physique and pleasing countenance. "I'm First Officer Donato Dellaguarda. Passengers aren't allowed on my Bridge."

He noted Dominick's broad shoulders, muscles and firm thighs, not to mention his thick black curly hair and deep bearishly black eyes. "But in this case, I'll make an exception. What may I do for you?"

Dominick stated his name, and handed the officer a letter from the Senator's office.

"Chief Detective O'Malley of the Brooklyn PD asked me to introduce myself." He handed the officer another note requesting access to the wireless telegraph room. "Our New York Senator and Police Commissioner request the captain and crew's full cooperation for a murder investigation."

"I see," Donato said as he read the letters. "A murderer aboard? One of the opera stars? This will be an exciting voyage, after all." Dominick noticed that the man's sea green eyes flashed as he brushed a long black curl from his forehead. "I'll take care of this personally."

Another officer called that the ship was headed for an oil tanker ahead. "It'll move out of our way—we're bigger." Donato confidently called out some compass directions, and the ship's course was set.

"Who drove this ship outta the dock and steered us through The Narrows?" Dominick asked in alarm.

"That would be me," Donato said proudly.

"Whadda ya know, you're an amazing driver!" Dominick slapped him on the back broadly. "I'm sure it ain't easy to get this tug of lard to maneuver."

"Thank you. However, the correct term is pilot the ship, and as for 'tub of lard', well, this ship is the most streamlined and well designed luxury cruise liner ever built. She's designed for speed, and does —"

"28.92 knots," Dominick finished for him.

"And you should see her in rough weather," Donato laughed.

"You should be our captain," another officer said.

"One day I'll get the title that comes with 'driving this tub of lard,' as you put it."

"But we're stuck with party boy Bevilacqua," the other officer said.

Dominick walked over to the machinery and started to pull a throttle.

"Hey, don't touch the controls! This ship has the latest technology. Those spinners suck in sea water to stabilize her. You almost sent us to list sideways!" Donato admonished him.

"There," he thrust the lever back to stable. "I'd better show you the telegraph room." They walked into an adjacent room.

"What's this?" Dominick pointed to a series of buttons and knobs. "If I want to relay a message? I push this button?"

"You can push my button anytime," Donato playfully suggested. "It does get lonely when one spends most of one's days in the middle of the big blue ocean, with nothing but the fish."

Dominick asked, "Don't you go ashore?" Wondering if any crew members had been to the opera, he asked, "Where were you last night?"

"I thought I'd hang out in Greenwich Village. Delightful place. I was at the Tosta Caffé, but the coffee in New York just isn't up to par with our coffee in Trieste."

"What about later, around 11 pm?"

I went to the Humped Camel to listen to some Jazz. Real music, not that opera stuff. A real dive bar. Full of people from all over. You don't find that in Italy. What a roaring time we had."

He paused to study Dominick again. "I can show you a great bar in Naples, along the waterfront."

A long loud blast echoed from the oil tanker as the *SS Rex* briskly passed it by.

"That's an American oil company tanker headed to Alicante to Franco's refineries," Donato said. "The US companies keep supplying Spain's fascist war effort. They have no allegiances."

Dominick wondered if supplying Franco was forbidden under the Neutrality Act. He'd read about the act which passed in July.

"Isn't sending oil to the Spanish Fascists forbidden?"

"Nope. Franco has a large credit line with the Americans. Oil follows wherever there's money. Amazing what you see out here in the ocean."

Captain Bevilacqua made his entrance. Dominick was surprised to find that he was young, boyish almost, of short stature with shaggy long blond hair, blue eyes, and looking somewhat peevish and foolish.

"I'm here now, boys," the captain announced. "Let's rev up those engines—full speed ahead!"

"No, men," said Donato. "There are a lot of container ships in the channel. Moderate speed until we hit deeper blue."

The mates looked from one to the other, then followed Donato's orders.

The captain shrugged and called for an orange juice spritzer with Prosecco.

"Captain Bevilacqua, I'm Dominick Abitello and I need to speak with you urgently." Dominick showed his missives from the Brooklyn PD and the Senator.

"A murderer aboard! My officers will give you full cooperation. First Officer Donato here will take charge."

Donato rolled his eyes.

They were interrupted by the beeping of a telegraph machine, and an officer came forward. "Are you Dominick? There's a message just come through for you. It doesn't make much sense, though."

Dominick had written out a code book for the Chief Detective before he set sail, so the two could communicate in secret.

Dominick strode to the telegraph room to decode the brief message. "FDR's Neutrality Act enacted, stop. Check ship for arms smuggling, stop. Report back on murder suspects, stop."

He folded the telegram and decided not to say anything about the first two parts of the message. He told the telegraph operator to radio a reply saying "Received."

He returned to the Bridge, and spoke to Captain Bevilacqua.

"Sir, I'll need to begin interviewing the murder suspects."

"Oh, yes, of course, you'll have our full cooperation. And I know just how to start your investigation. I'll invite the opera stars to sit at my table for dinner tonight." He called to another officer. "Giuseppe, send invitations to the staterooms. I must go and get ready for the festivities. Carry on." He smoothed his hair then grabbed his captain's hat from a peg, smartly cocking it to the side as he left the Bridge.

Dominick looked at the telegram and was confused. What did the Neutrality Act have to do with a murder at the opera? Now O'Malley wanted him to check for armaments aboard, as if he didn't have enough to do?

Dominick turned to Donato, who was back at the wheel. He seemed like an intelligent, educated man, so he ventured a question.

"Have you heard of FDR's Neutrality Act?"

"The US Neutrality Act prohibits the export of arms, ammunition, and implements of war from the United States to belligerent nations, and requires arms manufacturers in the United States to apply for an export license. Americans will no longer be able to board ships from any belligerent nation."

"So, does that mean Italian ships?"

"Not yet. Probably means German ships, I think. But there'll be an exception, of course, a 'cash and carry' for those countries that can pay cash for arms."

"Which countries?"

"That's Britain and France, of course. Italy can hardly afford tanks or even a cache of rifles."

"Maybe Mussolini can get credit somehow, like Franco."

"Maybe."

Donato ordered the ship to full speed ahead as they left the channel. He gripped the wheel, steering the ship through the heavy chop and calling out compass directions to set the course for Gibraltar.

Satisfied that he could break a new record, he set the autopilot rope, then turned to Dominick.

"See you at dinner?"

Dominick nodded and left the Bridge.

Chapter 8 - Saltzie's Stateroom

S altzie patted the loveseat, but Josephine refused to sit down. "I'm not here to play footsie," she said. "Let's find out what's in that bottle. Now pull it out of your pants and hand it over."

Saltzie pretended to swoon.

"Please, Josephine, come closer to administer mouth to mouth and pound on my chest, like the bearcat you are."

"Bottle first."

He reached in his pocket and pulled out the glass bottle.

She excitedly went to fetch it, and put it on the table. Feeling she owed him a kiss, they embraced; then as the ship hit a wave, they rolled onto the floor in a tangle.

"We're not going to get anywhere like this, if you keep trying to make love to me."

"But—I wasn't, really. It was the ship."

Josephine ran out of the stateroom, calling over her shoulder, "I'll find Maria and Antonio. They'll keep you in line."

The door slammed leaving Saltzie sitting on the floor, exasperated.

Josephine walked down the hallway past a giant wall papier-maché map of the Atlantic Ocean, with a relief of the coasts of America to the west and Europe to the east. The ship's ports of call in

New York, Gibraltar, Nice, Genoa and Naples were indicated by stars. Being slid on a wire across its trajectory was a model of the *SS Rex*. It was already out into the open ocean. *Oh, dear! This ship better slow down!*

Josephine descended one side of the imperial grand staircase, which unfolded before her like a tapestry, and as the ship moved, she clung to the iron balustrades, weaving her fingers in between its Neoclassical patterns, and the inlaid marble floors looked even more dizzyingly ornate. The ship began to rock from side to side. Josephine wavered as she found her way down to the grand lobby.

I'll never find Maria and Antonio. The ship is too big and it's moving too much. I can hardly walk. She spotted a purser at his station. "Excuse me, I'm trying to find my friends. Would you page them for me?"

The purser looked startled. "Say, aren't you Dr. Josephine Reva? I'm from Brooklyn, too. Just like you. You solved that case back in 1929—the Aconite murders. I read all about it. I recognize you from your photo in the newspaper. What a photo!" He whistled. "There were a lot of guys swooning for you when you were in jail. The Poison Femme Fatale."

"I didn't do any poisoning, and I caught the murderer," Josephine said. But she realized it would be good to have someone on the ship who knew its ins and outs, so she smoothed her hair and batted her blue eyes at the purser. "It's nice of you to notice. Can you help me find my friends?"

"Sure thing, Miss Queen of Poisons," he said. "Would you give me your autograph, please?"

"Here," she said taking one of his messenger cards and writing a few flirty lines, then signing with a doctor's scrawl.

The porter accepted the card, but practically crossed his eyes trying to read it. She took another card and tried to write Maria and Antonio's names clearly. "Please page these people for me and tell them to meet me on A Deck in Dr. Saltzman's stateroom."

"Yes, Dr. Reva. Yes, ma'am!"

He took up his silver tray, placed the message card on it, rang a bell and called out, incorrectly: "Marie and Antonello Collo."

Josephine shrugged and climbed back up the great staircase, grasping the railing. She noted how elegantly the other passengers were dressed; the women in smart dresses with fox collars and the men in their pinstripes. She looked down at her own simple dress and shoes, and realized she should have asked the Brooklyn PD for extra money to buy a First Class wardrobe to go with her First Class ticket. *Next time Chief Detective O'Malley needs my help, I'll ask for the moon.*

Walking towards the ship's papier-maché map again, she spotted Lady Montague and Lord Capulet whispering angrily together. She hid behind a column, but unfortunately, they heard her approach. Turning quickly, they went their separate ways.

Josephine found her way back to Saltzie's cabin, just as Maria and Antonio were arriving.

"Wowzer! What a fancy stateroom!" said Antonio upon entering. "It's bigger than our living room." He opened the sliding door to the outside. "Would you look at this balcony! What a view!"

"You could fitta table for ten out here," said Maria. She walked back inside and continued oohing and aahing. "And look, the bathroom even has a tub!"

Saltzie excitedly showed Josephine the chemistry lab he'd set up on the dining table. "A present for you!"

Josephine kissed him.

"You two scientists get to work," Antonio called to Josephine and Saltzie, "while Maria and I step outside to enjoy the moonlight."

Josephine and Saltzie leaned over the apparatus and set about testing the bottle's content.

"There's not much remaining. Which poison should we test for first, Joe?"

"Let's test for what we believe is the most likely botanical poison —Belladonna."

"OK, there's enough sample in the bottle."

"Saltzie, do we have any hair samples from Juliet's scalp?"

"Let me check my cufflinks. They got caught in her hair and I may have pulled a few strands out." He went to his dresser. "Lucky for us, I never had time to polish them in my rush to make the ship. Ah ha, here's one."

"Great, let's segment this and test. I hope you pulled it out from the root."

They gathered their liquids and set to work.

"We can incubate these in 1mL of phosphate buffer in the presence of atropine and scopolamine."

They took the residue and reconstituted then eluted it with a flow rate of 0.2 mL/min.

"Did you bring a Quattro Micro triple-quadrupole mass spectrometer?"

"You know, I always carry one."

Ionization was achieved using electro-spray in the positive mode.

"I've identified scopolamine in these segments, in the range 14 to 48 pg/mg.," Josephine announced.

"No doubt about it—it's reactive with the agent," Saltzie agreed. They looked at each other.

"It's *Atropa belladonna.*"

"But look! There's a solid at the bottom of the bottle, too." Josephine took a drink stirrer and began scraping residue along the edges. She examined it closely. "It's almost glowing—a very pretty blue-green."

"Maybe it's just contaminant from the leaves of the Belladonna plant."

"Why don't we perform a jar test, just to be sure."

She went to Saltzie's complimentary martini bar and rummaged through it, finding an olive jar. She poured out the contents, to Saltzie's protestations, and then cleaned the jar.

She then poured in the rest of the poison bottle's strange compound, and replaced the lid.

"Let this sit in the sunlight for a few days."

Josephine went out onto the balcony, startling Maria and Antonio from their passionate lover's embrace. Josephine smiled at them, then put the jar down on the balcony table, seating it within a ring meant to hold a drinks glass. "We're conducting another test."

"Did we hear Saltzie call you *Bella donna*, beautiful woman?" asked Maria. "Are you finally engaged?"

"Better than that, our tests showed that the poison in the bottle was indeed Belladonna," she replied.

"Oh, is tat all," Maria said. "I was hoping—"

There was a rustling sound.

A large bright gold envelope was being pushed under the stateroom door.

Saltzie went to open it as the others gathered around.

He read aloud the ornately scrolled announcement card:

INVITATION TO THE CAPTAIN'S TABLE
Dinner to be served at 20:00 hours
For 1st Class Passenger Dr. Charles A. Saltzman
+1 Guest

"Plus one guest?" Josephine asked him.

"You're my guest, of course."

"Why didn't I receive my own invitation?"

"The first night at the Captain's Table is for selected passengers. It's quite an honor.

"Don't worry," Saltzie continued, "I'm sure the captain is dying to meet you. After all, you're a famous poisoner."

"And you're a famous bootlegger."

"Now, *ragazzi*, kids, stop competing with each other," Antonio said. "Go get ready for a nice romantic dinner together."

"We're gonna have to keep pushing tese two," Maria whispered to her husband, "if they're ever gonna get married."

"If they don't throw each other overboard first."

Chapter 9 - Dinner at the Captain's Table

The conversation in the First Class Dining Salon echoed across the lush marble wall tiles and columns. Glowing electric lights were hidden inside the double-height tray ceilings with their heavy coffered beams, giving a candlelight effect. The floors were a striking symmetry of black and white diamonds, a stunning contrast to the green of the marble and sumptuous paintings of Italian landscapes.

Waiters scurried to and fro, throwing white tablecloths like sails unfurling in the breeze. They placed these over circular tables surrounded by plush armchairs in rounded conversation style. The four course dinner was meant to savor at leisure, until guests would head to the adjacent ballroom.

The Captain's long table set for twelve was placed in the most commanding spot surrounded by an archway, and two huge brass urns stood at each end with palms fronds and flowers.

Josephine and Saltzie found their place cards opposite a couple dressed in unusual evening wear. Josephine recognized them as the designer friends of Henrietta Porter-Graves.

The dark-haired woman wore a crisp white, heavily structured gown with an asymmetrical peaked shoulder, and her bodice had a bright red enormous crab appliquéd. The crab's claws were positioned one around each of her breasts. The pincers, one imagined, pinched her nipples.

"Isn't it shocking?" the woman announced loudly to Josephine, pointing at the pincers. "It's my latest creation—I'm sure the fashion magazines will take notice."

"It'll sell," said the man to Saltzie. "For gads of money. The more outrageous the better. Celebrities will be stupid enough to even wear it."

"I resent that. It's a beautiful gown."

"It's a beautiful gown, with a crab on it." The man laughed uproariously, and she joined in, tilting her head back.

"I'm in a nautical, or should I say naughty, mood," she laughed even harder.

"Crabs, get it?" The man asked Josephine and Saltzie, who looked on with appalled expressions.

"This is hardly appetizing," whispered Saltzie.

The man was dressed not in a dinner jacket, but in a flowing blue cape with a black beret tilted on his head. One could almost imagine him holding a palette and paintbrush.

Josephine lifted her eyebrows towards Saltzie as the two took their seats.

"We're seated with a couple of Italian lunatics," he whispered. "Hardly the romantic dinner I was expecting."

"Remember, we need to spy on the opera stars," whispered Josephine.

"Isabella Schiavone," the woman introduced herself, shaking Josephine's and Saltzie's hands. "And this is my good friend and inspiration, Fernando Delitto, the famous artist."

"I'm not a painter, but a sculptor, as you probably know," Fernando said. "Did you catch my latest exhibition at the Whitney Museum on Fifth? It was a smashing success."

Josephine said no, but Saltzie looked at the man. "You're not the one who creates those jelly sculptures?"

"Jelly?" Delitto harrumphed. "No, it's a combination of beeswax and plaster on form. A morph of residue that I melt and sculpt around a wire shape with my own two hands."

"Very interesting," said Saltzie. "I am something of a sculptor myself. Of the human body, though. I'd love to know the chemical composition of the castings—do you use any botanicals?"

The two began a conversation about this.

Isabella faced Josephine. "That's, um, a sweet dress you have on. Flutter sleeves—how quaint."

"A friend made it for me. I'm not a fashionista."

"I can see that," Isabella said scathingly. "But not to worry. You've got a nice shape. Reva, like in Venice? Are you Italian?"

"Yes, both my parents were. But I was born in New York."

"Pure blood, excellent. That's why you have symmetrical bone structure. I love your bosom. You must let me decorate it." She motioned with her hands around Josephine's form. "A white bodice, with perhaps some squids shooting black ink." She snickered.

Josephine managed to look enthusiastic. "Oh, I'd love that."

"Better than those silly little flowers around your neckline," Isabella continued. "What are they—weeds?"

"No, they're Belladonna berries—do you know the plant? It's one of my favorite medicinals."

"Never heard of it," snorted Isabella. "Plants don't interest me. I'm in my sea creature period."

"I wonder who else is at the dinner table," Josephine continued.

"There's our gorgeous young captain, you know he's the son of one of Naples' richest families, an eligible Blond Boy Bachelor. And the Confituras and the Arrabias, they're nobility, of course. And that's the ship's doctor, Karl Mahlberg, he's a German, very well-trained—you're both doctors, too, aren't you?"

"I'm a General Practitioner and Dr. Saltzman is a GI specialist."

"I heard you tried to save Freda, that poor girl. Such a tragedy. I can't imagine why she'd kill herself when she had so much to live for."

"Yes, very sad. Perhaps she didn't commit suicide. Do you have any idea who might have wanted her dead?"

"Murdered? That's ridiculous. She was well-loved," Isabella retorted, taking a drag of her cigarette and blowing smoke in Josephine's face. "Why are you on this luxury cruise?"

"We're going on vacation. I sing, amateur opera, that is. It's our first trip to Italy."

"How sweet. And your husband? He's a fine looking creature."

"No, we're just dating."

"Oh, you must get on with it. Children, no time to waste. We are all expected to do our part for Italy."

"Oh, do you have children?"

"No, of course not. I'm too busy. My job is to create fashion. The more obscene and shocking, the better. You don't have any creative talent, I can see that." She stubbed out her cigarette in the bread dish.

"But I have an important job, too. I save people."

"I suppose that's something, although I don't know why anyone would want to do that."

"There are a few empty chairs," Josephine said. "I wonder who else is coming to dinner?"

"How should I know?" Isabella turned to take another cigarette from Fernando.

"Wowee, these two are obnoxious," Josephine whispered to Saltzie.

"Horrid," he replied. "But Delitto knows how to make chemical mixtures."

"Isabella is a snob. I think she's a fascist, too. But she doesn't believe Juliet was murdered."

They turned to the table directly in front of theirs, also a table for honored guests. Josephine waved to Dominick, Maria, Antonio and the Porter-Graves. Olivia had made sure to sit next to Dominick. Around the circular table were also seated Cardinal Schlummer, the Devil's Advocate, Friar Lawrence, and the opera's Nurse.

The captain made sure to flit between tables, to welcome all the important VIPs on the voyage.

Josephine hoped that Dominick, Maria and Antonio would be able to engage the others at their table in conversation. She caught Maria's attention, raised her menu to subtly point to the suspects. Maria nodded.

Meanwhile, another guest had taken a seat at the Captain's Table, to Josephine's left.

A man with silver hair, wearing a starched white collar and well-cut dinner jacket, greeted her with a polite British accent.

"Sir Lucian Jones. Pleased to make your acquaintance, young lady. I'll be getting off at Gibraltar."

"Dr. Josephine Reva. Pleased as well. So you won't be continuing on to France and Italy?" She mentally ticked off all the stamps that would be added to her new passport, which Detective O'Malley had rush ordered the day before.

"No, New York was chaotic enough for me. I don't know how you Americans can stand all that noise and the crowds." He took a sip of wine and began to eat.

Josephine noted that there was still an empty chair, opposite the captain in the place of honor.

She asked Isabella who was still a no show.

"*Ah! La Bella Figura,*" she replied.

"What do you mean?"

"*La Bella Figura* is an Italian saying for the most beautiful and well-dressed. Always the last to arrive. You know, beauty is the most important characteristic of all."

"Being beautiful doesn't mean that a person has any goodness of character," Josephine frowned. "More often it's the opposite."

Sir Lucian nodded. "Indeed. Well said, Dr. Reva."

Isabella sniffed. "Presentation is everything. I suppose you don't judge a book by its cover, either."

"No, not really. I read medical journals."

Josephine noticed that Dominick, Maria and Antonio had turned their chairs and were leaning forward to speak to Captain Bevilacqua and the Montagues. Every so often, they all laughed uproariously.

I do hope they're talking about Fascism, but it doesn't appear so. How am I ever going to find out who killed Juliet?

Wait staff appeared, and the first course was served. Josephine enjoyed the consommé soup and the hors d'oeuvres of shrimp and caviar canapés.

Captain Bevilacqua commanded the helm of the table with his jovial banter throughout the dinner. If nothing else, one could say that he knew how to entertain, if not how to pilot a ship. He kept the champagne flowing and gave saucy winks to all the ladies present, promising he would dance with them all.

To the captain's left sat Lord and Lady Capulet, who were still very quiet in their grief, then Ferdinand Delitto, Isabelle Schiavone, and Dr. Mahlberg, the ship's doctor.

To the captain's right, and nearest to Dominick's table, were Lord and Lady Montague, then Saltzie, Josephine and Sir Lucian.

The empty seat remained empty, even after the last course was served. Josephine wondered if *"La Bella Figura"* was a man or a woman, or if the person would even show up.

Just then, Mrs. Porter-Graves came over. She was wearing a white structured gown, one of Isabella Schiavone's latest creations, with a gigantic mossy appliqué of an oyster emitting a black pearl across the front, over where her uterus would be.

"Shocking, isn't it?" Henrietta laughed, pointing to the oyster. "Of course, Olivia is my pearl. I absolutely love it, Isabella."

"So glad *you* do." She winked at Mr. Delitto, who laughed as if the two were sharing a private joke.

Sir Lucian was speaking with Dr. Mahlberg across the table, and their voices grew louder.

"As we speak, Mussolini gets ready to launch an invasion into Abyssinia," said Sir Lucian. "There's talk he may defy the Geneva Protocols and use that horrid mustard gas.We must defend that poor country, and impose tough sanctions on Italy and Germany for their belligerence. Only then may we be able to prevent another Great War. The League of Nations is nothing but a scrap of paper if we don't have the courage of our convictions."

"Sanctions do little when they don't include oil, gas and coal. American ships will continue to supply Franco's regime. Germany will find its own source."

"Mussolini must not spill black Abyssinian blood! The League must be color blind. Ethiopia is a member of the League. An invasion against one is an invasion against all."

"But Ethiopian blood is the cheaper commodity. We need oil, gas and coal. How will we heat our homes, run our machines and build great ships like this one? The French and British will not oppose Italy's invasion into Abyssinia, even if Mussolini uses mustard gas. And the US will keep making exceptions to sell arms, oil, gas and coal to the Italians, no matter what Il Duce does. That's so-called neutrality."

"At least, Germany will have to fend for itself. The Treaty of Versailles forbids Hitler's re-armament."

"Not for long," Dr. Mahlberg smiled.

Mrs. Porter-Graves was aghast and interrupted the men. "It is a curious thing—we desire peace and want to avoid war, but as soon as there's talk of money, we make concessions. Whatever happens, some people insist that their pockets be lined."

"Well said," Sir Lucian replied.

Captain Bevilacqua arose from his chair, raising his champagne coupe.

"Un brindisi, speech!" the Italian passengers called out, noting that only the uncouth Americans were clinking their lead crystal water glasses with their spoons.

"What a fantastic ship our SS Rex is!" said the captain. "She's built for speed and we'll race across the Atlantic. We won the Blue

Riband and held the title from 1933-until this summer, with the fastest crossings ever. *Viva l'Italia!*"

"*Viva l'Italia!*" The passengers repeated.

"On this journey, we shall retake our crown! Our speed eastbound, without encountering any rough weather, is expected to be 25.9 knots. For the return, we are aiming for full speed of 29 knots! A new record! *Bravo Mussolini! Vincere e vinceremo!*"

The passengers cheered and began singing a national song.

"Good. The sooner I can get to Gibraltar, the better," remarked Sir Lucian to Josephine. "These fascists are too boisterous and bellicose. If they invade Abyssinia, it'll be the downfall of us all."

A wall panel in the dining room was slid open, revealing a ball room. Framed by massive squared columns in the classical style, the ballroom's walls were covered in opulent moldings, Trompe-l'œil windows and balconies in the romantic style. There was a large stage set up high, an orchestra already striking up a tune, and a large dance floor surrounded by tables. There were exclamations of glee from the passengers.

Captain Bevilacqua took the hand of Lady Capulet. "Shall we dance?" He was expertly trying to help her recover from her tragic loss, and she sighed, then accepted his offer. He then shepherded her to the dance floor. The two expertly fox-trotted.

Other diners followed the pair to the ballroom and began dancing.

Lord Capulet watched for a bit, then turned away. Josephine and Saltzie tried to engage him in conversation, but he was too pensive.

Dr. Mahlberg was intently staring at Saltzie's profile. "What is Saltzie the diminutive of?" he asked.

"Saltzman."

"Does that mean 'a man who sells salt?'"

"Sort of."

"Ahh, I see, a Hebrew name." The doctor then seemed to be examining Saltzie's head and face. He took a long look at Saltzie's ears as if measuring them.

Saltzi grew uncomfortable, and he spoke up. "You know, being Jewish in New York City is seen as an attribute."

The ship's doctor sniffed.

Lady Montague interjected. "Ah, ha! I knew there was a reason why you're so intelligent. Jews make excellent doctors."

Saltzie wasn't sure if he should be offended, or if her remark was meant as a compliment. He decided it was the former, and sank lower in his chair. He didn't feel up to asking Josephine for a dance.

Lord Montague asked permission of Antonio, then extended his hand to Maria to dance, and Lady Montague then danced with Antonio. Fernando Delitto danced with Isabella Schiavone. Dr. Mahlberg asked Josephine, who with a nod to Saltzie, declined, so he went and cut in on Fernando and Isabella. With the next song, the partners changed, and Captain Bevilacqua asked Henrietta to dance. She shook her head, so the captain held out his hand for Olivia. Pointing to her leg, she refused, but the captain was not one to take no for an answer. He cajoled and winked at her, as if pleading, until Olivia laughed. She got up and did her best to dance with him slowly. The captain gallantly made sure she didn't fall.

Dominick stood and watched enviously, then cut in on the pair. Holding Olivia tightly, he led her in a simple two step, as the other dancers swirled more briskly around them. He didn't mind at all.

After a few dances, everyone exchanged partners again. With all the swirling and lively dancing, the dancers became a blur of jewels and color until it wasn't possible to tell who was dancing with whom.

Midnight soon tolled on the ship's clock.

After a few minutes, Dr. Mahlberg begged off from more dancing. He said he'd go smoke a cigar before he was back on duty in the medical cabin for the night.

"Good riddance," said Saltzie. "That doctor gives me the creeps. Did you see the way he was examining my nose and ears?"

"Yes, he's a Nazi, for sure."

"I don't know which are worse, the Fascists or Nazis," said Saltzie glumly.

Lord Capulet and Sir Lucian also left, saying they were too tired for such revelry and would retire to their staterooms.

Suddenly, the happy chattering in the grand ballroom ceased.

An elegantly dressed man entered, and all eyes followed him. The man was not too tall, not too short, not too fat, not too thin, not too old, not too young. He was dressed in a meticulously tailored white evening jacket with white ascot, and a flaming red pocket handkerchief. Handsome, with a finely chiseled face, his regard was one of disdain. He sported a white felt fedora with a small dove feather in the black band, nattily tilted over one eye.

La Bella Figura, Josephine gasped. The distinguished gentleman carried a silver tipped walking stick and made his way arrogantly to the Captain's Table. Alfredo was trailing behind him more like a puppy rather than a famous tenor.

La Bella Figura stopped at the now vacant seat opposite Josephine and Saltzie, and Alfredo rushed to pull out a chair for him to sit down.

"*Buona sera,* good evening," the elegant man said. "My name is Ernesto Cacciavolpe. Dr. Josephine Reva and Dr. Charles Saltzman, I presume."

"*Buona sera,*" Josephine replied. "How do you know our names?"

"There's not much that escapes me," replied La Bella Figura, removing his fedora. His hair was thick and dark brown, and his eyes were deep pools of black that gave nothing away. He regarded Josephine intensely. "You are searching for the killer of Juliet. But you are confused."

"We were in the audience when it happened," said Saltzie. "We saw it all."

"Maybe you can tell us why she had to die," Josephine challenged.

"Ah, that is the one thing I do not know," he replied. "But I'm sure the answer will be revealed little by little, how would you say, like peeling the petals off of a flower."

"And what flower would that be?" she asked. "Belladonna?"

He got up. "Excuse me, *signorina, signore.* I'm going out on the Promenade Deck to take some air."

Alfredo remained at the table. Olivia plunked down next to him, exhausted. Alfredo sadly poured more champagne and toasted with Olivia.

The captain came back to the table excitedly. "We're pushing the engines to full speed tonight. I'm sure the voyage will take less than six days. A new record!"

Josephine frowned. She needed the ship to go slower, not faster.

Couples on the dance floor spun by, as the ship rocked on the waves. Olivia was chatting with Captain Bevilacqua, who took her hand and convinced her to dance again to a slower tune.

Donato had now left the Bridge and entered the ballroom. He noticed Dominick frowning as he watched Captain Bevilacqua holding Olivia tightly, the two dancing very closely.

Donato came alongside Dominick. "Leave it, there's no stopping our *capitano* once he starts flirting." Putting a hand on Dominick's chest to stop him from cutting in. "Jealousy is not a pretty face. Let's go outside for some air. I'll show you the view from the Bridge at night." He grabbed a bottle of Prosecco, and the two left the ballroom.

The music stopped, and all the couples applauded.

Captain Bevilacqua led Olivia to a chair, then stepped forward to make another announcement.

"*Signore e signori*, Ladies and Gentleman, we are pleased that our famous opera divas and dons from Mussolini's opera troupe are aboard with us for our voyage. Perhaps we can persuade them to perform?" Everyone cheered.

He looked at the tenor Alfredo, but the young man sadly shook his head. "*Mi dispiace*, please excuse me. I'm not able to celebrate tonight."

"We have then Signore Arrabia, whose magnificent baritone thrilled Brooklyn audiences as Lord Montague in Romeo and Juliet. If you would be so kind."

Lord Montague nodded, but added that he would be honored if the "Brooklyn amateur" Antonio would join him. Antonio jumped up eagerly.

"Something lively," Antonio told the orchestra, "and everyone please do sing along!" He waved at all the passengers in the ballroom.

The orchestra struck up the notes to the song "Funiculì, Funiculà."

Antonio smiled at Maria, and then turned to the ballroom and spread his arms wide. Together with Lord Montague, the two baritones began singing:

Aissèra, oje Nanniné, me ne sagliette,
tu saje addó, tu saje addó
Addó 'stu core 'ngrato cchiù dispietto
farme nun pò! Farme nun pò!
Addó lu fuoco coce, ma se fuje
te lassa sta! Te lassa sta!
E nun te corre appriesso, nun te struje
sulo a guardà, sulo a guardà.

I climbed up high this evening, oh, Nanetta,
Do you know where? Do you know where?
Where this ungrateful heart
No longer pains me! No longer pains me!
Where fire burns, but if you run away,
It lets you be, it lets you be!
It doesn't follow after or torment you
Just with a look, just with a look.

The passengers joined in for the chorus, twirling and tossing their napkins in the air. *These white napkins in flight look like a flock of seagulls*, thought Josephine.

Slowly, she began singing in her clear mezzo-soprano. Soon she was clapping her hands to the joyful beat, then took up her white napkin, too, waving it back and forth like the others.

Jamme, jamme 'ncoppa, jamme jà,
Jamme, jamme 'ncoppa, jamme jà,
funiculì, funiculà, funiculì, funiculà,
'ncoppa, jamme jà, funiculì, funiculà!

Let's go, let's go! To the top we'll go!
Let's go, let's go! To the top we'll go!
Funicular up, funicular down,
funicular up, funicular down!
To the top we'll go, funicular up, funicular down!

Lady Capulet and Lady Montague were moved by the uplifting song. They embraced and exclaimed that they forgave each other, crying on one another's shoulder.

Josephine watched them with curiosity as she continued singing. It was odd to see such such an outpouring of emotion from the two divas, who normally were at odds with each other.

Satlzie and the other Americans stared in shock at the emotive Italian passengers, who were now dancing around Antonio and Lord Montague, begging them for an encore.

"What's all this about?" he asked Josephine.

Josephine explained that the song was written to commemorate the opening of a funicular to take visitors to the top of Mount

Vesuvius, an engineering marvel for the 1800's. But the song also had a deeper significance; the lyrics told the heartwarming story of a young man who compares his undying love for his sweetheart to climbing the volcano, and invites her to join him at the summit.

"But that's so dangerous," Saltzie said. "I wouldn't go anywhere near a spewing volcano."

"Oh, I think it's so romantic," Josephine replied. Then she turned to Saltzie. "Now aren't we a pair? Before, you were the risk-taking romantic one, and me, the voice of reason. Now it seems we're becoming the opposite!"

"Maybe it's this crazy voyage." He pointed to the crowd waving their white napkins, as the ship rocked on the harder waves. "You're finding your Neapolitan streak, and I'm here to protect you."

"From the murderer?"

"From any harm."

"It's this undercover work," sighed Josephine. "Me, an amateur opera singer? I know, it's crazy, but this voyage brings out another side of me. I haven't felt this way since I was a young girl, when Mother Cabrini inspired me. I felt like I could achieve anything I set out to do."

"Maybe you're feeling fiery because we're getting closer to the volcano?"

"Now that's a danger. I can feel it in my bones that something terrible is going to happen. It must be the lava raising my blood pressure."

"Well, I like the new adventurous Dr. Reva. Please stay this way. Vesuvius or not."

They kissed more passionately, as the chorale chant of "Let's go to the top!" resounded in their ears.

"Why don't we head outside to look at the ocean," Josephine suggested, taking Saltzie's hand.

"Just what the doctor ordered."

The two left to stroll on the Promenade Deck in the moonlight.

Josephine and Saltzie saw Sir Lucian and Dr. Mahlberg standing at the railing, smoking cigars. Dr. Mahlberg left, and La Bella Figura then joined Sir Lucian. They watched Friar Lawrence and the Nurse stumble in drunken humor and drift away to their cabins.

Josephine and Saltzie laughed and linked arms, continuing their stroll, breathing in the fresh nighttime sea air.

Inside, the remaining passengers solemnly began singing the *Abyssinian Girl*. Its echoes drifted out the ballroom windows and surrounded the ship like a dark cloud.

"There's that song again," said Josephine. "Juliet sang it—"

"Those must be the diehard fools," Saltzie said in disgust.

Choruses soon echoed from everywhere—the ballroom, the Promenade Deck and down below in the lower classes.

"There are plenty of fascists on this boat," she shivered.

"Don't worry, I'm here for the entire voyage."

He took off his evening jacket and placed it around her shoulders.

They watched the moonlight dancing on the waves, then kissed some more. They then sat down next to each other on deck chairs, watching the stars and talking about their more unusual medical cases.

The revelers inside the ballroom sang many more songs, long into the night. It was soon 2 a.m., and the revelers repeated a more slurred version of *Funiculì, funiculà!*

But the song's joyous chorus was broken by a piercing scream. Josephine and Saltzie heard a thump and then a distinct splash in the ocean.

They raced to find its source, peering over the railing.

"There," said Josephine, pointing as the dark waves drew a body downward into the ocean's black depths.

Chapter 10 - Overboard

M AN OVERBOARD! MAN OVERBOARD!"
The purser shouted as he ran to an alarm bell and pulled it.

A loud whirring siren sounded.

The remaining guests from the Captain's Table rushed out the glass doors to the Promenade Deck, and leaned over the railing to search the dark waters.

"There!" Several passengers cried out, as they pointed towards crumpled clothing.

The ocean was tugging the body into a whirlpool, sucking it downward then releasing it to float on the waves. The corpse was face down.

Cries of "*Dio mio!* My God!" were heard repeatedly from the horrified passengers.

The engines of the massive ship ground to a halt and the ship drifted on the rough waves. Crewmen began lowering a lifeboat inch by inch, cautiously over the side.

Once in the water, they rowed until they reached the body, which had now drifted several hundreds of yards away.

"He's surely drowned by now," Josephine said.

Deckhands gaffed the body into the lifeboat and rowed back alongside the ocean liner. They turned the corpse over, revealing a water soaked face.

"It's Dr. Mahlberg," said Josephine.

The crewman felt for a pulse, but sadly said, "*E morto*. He's dead."

The nurse from the opera rushed forward, startled. "Why would he jump overboard?"

"He may have been pushed. We heard a thump," Josephine said. "Let's find where he fell from." Together, she and Saltzie followed the course of the railing. "Look, here's some fresh blood and hairs." She then pointed up to the deck above. "He must have been standing there on the upper Promenade, then fell and hit this railing. Maybe he bounced off it and fell into the water."

Captain Bevilacqua looked queasy. Donato took charge and barked some orders. Deckhands rushed to secure the area and collect evidence.

Donato whispered to Dr. Olivia Porter-Graves, who nodded and went to the deceased Dr. Mahlberg's medical suite. It was ironic, she thought, that it was his body that they would be examining for a Post Mortem in his own office.

Olivia walked past the rows of hydrotherapy inhalers set up for the passengers. Tuberculosis, depression, anxiety—hydrotherapy plus sea air was the most sought after treatment for all sorts of ailments.

She pulled on rubber gloves, folding them as tightly as possible around her hands, and picked up a large hacksaw, inspecting its blade.

Josephine and Saltzie soon entered with the deckhands lugging the sodden Dr. Mahlberg, wrapped within a dripping tarp.

"Put him on the table," Olivia said. "I know some people think that it's morbid for a woman to take pleasure in an autopsy, but I rather enjoy it."

"Josephine does, too, as I recall," winked Saltzie. "I, however, prefer my patients with some breath left in them."

"Dr. Mahlberg can't talk back, which is a relief," Josephine said, and the others nodded, remembering the doctor's decidedly Nazi leanings.

She tied on a rubber apron, put on gloves, and then inspected Dr. Mahlberg's head. "The blood has congealed here," Josephine pointed to the back of the doctor's scalp. "It's thickened around the wound. He received a blow cracking the skull. We found blood and hair on a ship's railing, just outside the First Class Dining Salon."

"He probably fell," Saltzie said. "But he did announce that he wanted a smoke. Maybe he simply dropped his cigar lighter and tumbled after it?"

"He was standing with Sir Lucian, smoking a cigar, about an hour before he fell," Josephine said. "Let's have a look at his insides." She picked up a long, sharp scalpel. "Would you assist me, Dr. Porter-Graves?"

Olivia smiled and began peeling off Dr. Mahlberg's wet clothing.

"I will happily leave you ladies to the gory details. Autopsies make me squeamish," Saltzie joked, exiting the medical suite. "I'm going to have a look for clues around the Upper Promenade Deck."

The two woman doctors began cutting into the cadaver, then prying the chest open with large retractors.

At that moment, Dominick burst through the door.

"Doc Joe, Olivia, I mean Dr. Porter-Graves, are you okay? I was on the Bridge when it happened, or I'd have knocked that murderer senseless."

"It's all right, Dominick," said Josephine. "We were never in any danger. Only the unfortunate Dr. Mahlberg."

"I wonder if Dr. Mahlberg was killed for his Nazi beliefs," said Olivia.

"Perhaps, like Juliet may have been killed because she was a fascist," said Josephine. "The autopsy will give us more information."

"The autopsy will take some time, so no need to stay," Olivia noticed that Dominick's face was turning grey while staring at the open chest cavity, from which she was pulling out the intestines like spaghetti. "I wouldn't want to spatter that handsome face of yours."

Dominick didn't know whether to be shocked by Olivia's directness, or pleased by her compliment. He recovered quickly. "Don't worry, I've seen this before on the battlefield. It's never pretty. I'd best be keeping my eye on you gals."

"How comforting, thank you," Olivia smiled at him.

"Dominick, why don't you go question the suspects who left dinner before Dr. Mahlberg fell overboard?" Josephine asked. "Lord Capulet, Lady Montague. I suppose the cardinal and Devil's Advocate weren't dancing, so they were missing. We saw Friar Lawrence and the Nurse together, then Sir Lucian on the Promenade Deck smoking a cigar just after midnight with Dr. Mahlberg. Then that man, *La Bella Figura*—he left, too."

"Anyone without an alibi will be confined to their cabins by the captain, I mean Donato's orders. Donato, as the captain's representative, has agreed to give us the crew's full cooperation. When I'm questioning the suspects in their cabins, I can look for any evidence of Juliet's murderer, too."

"Great idea. I suspect these two murders are related," said Josephine. "Oh yes, I saw Lady Montague and Lord Capulet earlier in the hallway. You could ask them why they were arguing."

Dominick headed for the door, then turned to speak to the women again.

"Please send for me when you're done and we'll reconvene." He eyed Olivia. "I'm in Interior Stateroom 202, B Deck." He patted his jacket, opening it to reveal a gun in a holster. "Old army issue. Please be careful, there's a murderer, maybe two murderers, aboard."

"We'll lock the door," Josephine said.

Olivia stole a glance at Dominick's tight derriere as he strode out the door.

Josephine noticed and smiled."Dominick is handsome, isn't he?"

"Like Clark Gable."

"There was a time I thought he looked like Rudy Valentino."

They shared a giggle before continuing the autopsy.

"A sharp blow to the head, and look, there's fresh bruising on his arms and neck," Josephine pointed to Dr. Mahlberg's skull and upper body

"He must have struggled with someone before he went over the railing. But he was face down in the ocean for over twenty minutes, and his lungs are full of seawater. Should we close him up? It looks like the cause of death was drowning."

"Wait, I'd like to see what's in his stomach," said Josephine. "We must be thorough, and I've a feeling we'll find something else."

They opened the organ to look at its ruminants.

"Dinner, of course. But see here: seeds, some fruit skins—these could be Belladonna berries!" exclaimed Josephine.

"There's a mighty foul odor, too."

"We've a lab in Saltzie's stateroom. I'll go test this matter, while you close. Keep your mask and gloves on."

"But why would someone poison the ship's doctor, then toss him overboard?"

"I don't know, but it seems someone is using Belladonna as a murder weapon."

Chapter 11 - Promenade Deck

Saltzie walked the Sports Deck of the upper promenade slowly scanning the ground. He was directly over the area where Dr. Mahlberg's blood had been found on the railing below. *I don't think that Nazi was up here swinging on the Trapeze or out for a midnight swim in the pool*, thought Saltzie. *He must have been meeting someone.* He continued searching the ground. *If I could find anything at all, like a cigarette butt, that might tell me who he was with.*

His eagle eyesight caught something glimmering next to the post. "Ah ha," he said aloud, and bent down. "A man's gold cufflink." He examined it to find some kind of insignia engraved on the face.

He wrapped it in his handkerchief carefully.

Rushing across the deck to find Josephine, he then realized she'd still be busy with the autopsy. But he spotted Dominick and Donato strolling. "I thought you two would be hard at work investigating."

"We've just had our *colazione,* breakfast and *espresso*," said Donato. "Naturally, we can't begin our work questioning the suspects until we're fully digested."

"Besides, they're confined to quarters, and can't escape." Dominick gestured to the vast expanse of ocean around them.

"Well, I've been investigating for both of you. Look, I found this."

Saltzie pulled out the gold cufflink. "It was over there at the bottom of the railing where Dr. Mahlberg was standing before he fell overboard. It surely belongs to the murderer."

"Maybe it's Dr. Mahlberg's?" Dominick asked. "And he lost it during the struggle or as he fell?"

"Mahlberg was a Nazi, and this insignia isn't a Swastika," Saltzie said.

"That's a *fascia*," said Donato. "It's the fascist emblem: a bundle of sticks. Alone they are weak and snap, but bound together they are strong."

"So whoever owns this cufflink is a fascist?" asked Dominick.

"Yes, it certainly appears so."

"See if you can find out who has the other cufflink of the pair," Saltzie said.

"We don't need you telling us what to do," huffed Dominick.

"Well, he did find an important piece of evidence," said Donato. Saltzie looked particularly proud.

"We can place whoever owns this cufflink at the scene of the crime," said Dominick, triumphantly.

Turning to Saltzie, he said, "We can take it from here."

"I'm glad to help. I could bring the cufflink to my stateroom and test it for fingerprints," said Saltzie.

Dominick held up the cufflink. "It looks like it's smudged. Is your lab good enough for that?"

Saltzie shrugged. "Probably not."

"We'll see if we can figure out the owner ourselves."

The trio continued along the Upper Promenade Deck to the Sports area, walking past the exercise equipment, trapeze, and shuffleboards, until they came to the large swimming pool. It was surrounded by real sand and beach umbrellas set up for the guests.

They stopped to watch the svelte form of the young woman who played Juliet's nurse as she sprung off the diving board. Friar Lawrence next did a somersault to impress her, and she was waving gaily to him as he surfaced.

"They're having fun," said Donato. "I don't like to disturb their little romance, but let's question them."

The three men approached the pool. The nurse and Friar Lawrence were busy dunking each other, then the friar dove under the nurse, pulled her legs over his shoulders and hoisted her above the water. They fell over together, laughing.

"*Mi scusate*, excuse me," said Donato. "Where were you two last night when Dr. Mahlberg fell overboard, about 2 a.m.?"

"We were dancing together until midnight, then left for my cabin," said the friar. "We only came up for air from our nookie when we heard the commotion."

"Yes, we were together the entire night," said the giggling nurse.

"Why did you remove evidence from the opera set?" asked Saltzie.

"Evidence?"

"Yes, the bottle Juliet drank from."

"I took it because that Chief Detective thought I poisoned her."

"No," said the nurse. "You don't need to cover for me. I found it under Juliet's bed and I didn't know what to do. I gave it to him."

"But then I lost it in a robbery in the alley. Then we couldn't say anything."

"It's alright. We found the bottle anyway." Saltzie was glad that the friar hadn't reported the crime.

The men walked on.

"Friar Lawrence is supposed to be helping us," moaned Dominick.

"Oh, let the young lovebirds be," said Donato.

"At least it's a romantic cruise for some people," Saltzie opined. "And would you look at Lady Capulet sitting over there under the beach umbrella with Lord Montague. Their bodies are very close together."

Lady Capulet got up and took off her swimming robe, unveiling her comely swimsuit form.

"She looks really good for her age."

"And Lord Montague can't peel his eyes off her," said Dominick. "Do you think they're having an affair?"

"It looks that way," said Donato.

Lady Capulet made an elegant swan dive into the pool.

Lord Montague watched, and after a few seconds, got up and dove in after her.

"Let's go question their spouses. I bet they're playing *switcheroo*," said Dominick. "Thanks for the cufflink clue," he told Saltzie. "Report back to us about the fingerprints."

"You know, Dom, someone's got to keep an eye on Josephine and Olivia to make sure they're safe. I'm glad to do so. Maybe they'd like a swim in the pool with me." With that he saluted the two men, and trotted off with a smile.

"That guy really irks me," said Dominick, as he and Donato headed towards the First Class Staterooms.

SOLIS MUNDI

Chapter 12 - Questioning the Suspects 2

E arly light illuminated Cardinal Schlummer and Father Della Pietra's stateroom. It was an ample suite for two priests, with two double beds, an outdoor balcony, and a large washroom with a bigger than typical tub on a trans-Atlantic liner.

The priests had called the porters to remove the unnecessary porcelain vases and Chinese tapestries. They had done their best to make the luxurious stateroom serviceable and spartan, then unpacked their numerous leather-bound volumes. In the armoire hung black cassocks, various robes, stoles, and upon a shelf sat a chalice for Eucharist. Fortunately, there was a chapel aboard the ship, so they left the confessional grill in its packaging.

On the dresser sat the ornate box they'd carried solemnly from New York containing Mother Frances Cabrini's relics.

Monsignor Della Pietra was seated at the desk, writing, He was pre-occupied. He'd been appointed *l'Advocato del Diavolo*, the Devil's Advocate without much deliberation. The matter was urgent; Mother Cabrini was such a popular candidate for sainthood that there wasn't anyone else who'd wanted to take the contrarian side and play Devil's Advocate.

Departing immediately from Rome, he'd set to work upon his arrival in New York and begun ordering interviews with witnesses. Now the reams of paperwork upon which his inquisition would be based were spread out like shifting sands upon his desk. To be a Devil's Advocate meant that he must doubt all the evidence and attempt to prove each statement wrong.

He looked at the first file about little baby Peter. What had happened in Columbus Hospital's maternity ward on that March night so long ago?

Wafting calls of albatross, which he admired, had ceased, but there were a few seagulls who had decided to hitch a ride on board for the journey. The noisy cawing as passengers fed them scraps of food unnerved him. He picked up one book, the memoirs of Mother Cabrini who had criss-crossed the Atlantic many times; she had commented on the seagulls, too, but to her they'd seemed messengers of God. Suspended in flight, their calls drifted in through her open porthole and called to her very soul. But to him, they seemed like pests.

He closed the book. *I must remain impartial.*

Yet he realized how important his findings would be. Were these would-be saints God's messengers or Devil's pawns? Monsignor Della Pietra's role was to disprove the miracles and expose them as the work of the Devil.

Was it so wrong to be a skeptic? Perhaps not wrong, but definitely unpopular.

With his tall, thin frame, his angular face and penetrating eyes, as a priest he more often frightened those he sought to comfort. Although his sermons had been eloquent, he had not gained a flock of devoted congregants—he had failed to inspire. He had never been able to show an unfailing submission to the teachings without a second's hesitation.

As a divinity student, his commentary on the gospels had been brilliant. He shared beliefs with his contemporaries, yet he remained always questioning.

Those impressed with his monk-like studiousness, had called him "the Unsatisfied", "*L'Insoddisfatto*". They had counseled him to stop searching for a sign of spiritual revelation.

"Hope is a desire based on fear," his mentor had said. "Revelation comes from belief."

Belief without question was his failing, the reason he had never moved from Monsignor to other posts in his diocese. Yet the Holy See had seen this as his strength, and chosen him as the man responsible for these most important inquiries into a missionary nun's benediction.

His position put him at odds with Cardinal Schlummer. The cardinal wanted to prove Mother Cabrini a saint quickly, perhaps more than he wanted to prove her not.

He had a role to fulfill, and he would be sure to do it, even if it put him at odds with most everyone.

The massive file lay open on the desk before him: letters, memoranda of a woman's life, from other's words, without flesh, without soul. A woman who in body had been frail, sickly. But this was no ordinary mortal, this was a missionary who had led an army of nuns across the Americas, unstoppable in her accomplishments in the name of the Holy Roman Catholic Church. She had founded and built 61 hospitals, schools, institutions—one for every single year that she had lived. She had converted or reinvigorated hundreds of thousands of Catholic Americans into the fold of the Church. At her death, she was mourned by millions of the faithful—they had filled masses and memorials and were calling for her rapid benediction. But the Papal ordinances stated that there must be a miracle, in fact, three miracles, that were proven Godly and not the work of the Devil.

Quickly, just a few years after her death, the first miracle occurred in one of her own hospitals.

Monsignor Della Pietra began to read through the eye witness accounts and the hundreds of letters from devoted nuns in Mother Cabrini's missionary. He read of her untiring work for the poor and downtrodden, and agreed that she was indeed a remarkable woman, but did that make her a Saint?

Cardinal Schlummer entered the stateroom, saying that he received a telegram last night.

"Papal orders, we are to speed up the canonization. Having an American Saint will help us convert more Americans. And we need to keep the Catholics interested and behind the Pope, especially if another war is coming."

Father DellaPietra turned angrily. "These things take years, decades even. We can't 'speed this up'."

The cardinal lambasted him. "You're such a Doubting Thomas! Can't you see that those miracles were divine intercession?"

"But we don't know if three miracles really did take place."

"Just get on with it and hurry! Whatever we do, we must keep these relics safe until she's proclaimed a saint."

There was a knock at the cabin door. Dominick and Donato entered and announced they were a search party investigating Dr. Mahlberg's murder.

Dominick walked to the dresser, noticing many gold items with *fascia* emblems. "Whose jewelry is all this?

"We both received gifts from Mussolini, for our important mission."

"Whose is this one?" He held up the found cufflink.

Cardinal Schlummer hesitated, but Father Della Pietra answered. "They're identical pairs. We keep them all together on the dresser, jumbled."

"We often wear *fascia* emblems—*fascia* means the weight we all must bear, the sticks, but we are stronger when bundled together," the cardinal added. "But did you say Dr. Mahlberg was murdered? I thought he fell."

"No, it appears he was attacked. And we found this cufflink at the railing where he last stood."

"That fascia emblem is a common one," the cardinal said. "Mussolini gives these out like candy to his admirers."

"May we examine your fingers." Donato looks at both hands, but finds nothing under their fingernails, and no signs of any bruising. "Washed."

"Yes, of course, we washed. Every morning, before communion and before handling the relic box."

"Let's see that relic box," Dominick said.

"Must you?"

Donato nodded. "Captain's orders."

The cardinal went to it and unlocked the lid with a skeleton key. "'See, only bones." Dominick looked inside. He tried to touch one of the bones, but the cardinal slapped his hand.

"Please don't touch! The bones are sacred."

"Sorry."

Meanwhile Donato had noticed an open nightstand drawer next to the cardinal's bed. He sidled over to it while the others were busy with the relics, and slid it open further. Empty.

Donato caught the attention of Dominick, who immediately realized what was missing. "Do you always travel without a Bible, Cardinal?"

"Mine is here somewhere. It's just been misplaced."

Dominick raised his eyebrow, and Donato nodded. The Devil's Advocate also noticed because he'd been watching Dominick. Now he looked at the First Mate with renewed interest.

"As for the cufflink," said the Devil's Advocate, "either of us could have dropped it anytime while walking on the Upper Promenade Deck for some much needed exercise."

"And Dr. Mahlberg? What was your acquaintance with him?" asked Donato.

"We didn't know Dr. Mahlberg. We didn't see him during the voyage and had no medical ailments."

"And what about Juliet, Miss Freda?" Dominick turned to Cardinal Schlummer.

"You already said you were her confessor, but did you have any other relationship?"

"Certainly not."

The Devil's Advocate looked at the cardinal, but said nothing.

Dominick and Donato left the prelates' stateroom in deep thought.

"We don't know if the gold cufflink belonged to the cardinal or the Devil's Advocate, nor when it was lost," Dominick began. "But one of them was most likely at the railing where Dr. Mahlberg died.

We know that the cardinal is a fascist and he doesn't know where his Bible is. He implied that there could be others with a Fascia cufflink. It's all suspicious, but it doesn't prove that either one of them killed Juliet or Dr. Mahlberg."

Donato said, "I think that Devil's Advocate knows much more than he's saying. I'd be sad if he proved to be the murderer. He's good looking and with that devilish demeanor—"

"Let's go speak with Sir Lucian. Josephine and Saltzie saw him smoking a cigar Dr. Mahlberg and later with that dandy, what did she call him, 'La Bella Figura'."

"That man does dress well. I'd like to have a look in his closet."

They found the largest state room on the highest deck, and knocked on the door. Sir Lucian was in a smoking jacket and greeting them holding a brandy and a cigar.

When they walked inside, they found La Bella Figura there as well. The two were apparently in the middle of a chess game.

"Check mate," said La Bella Figura, sliding his knight and knocking down Sir Lucian's King. "You shouldn't make it so easy for me." He puffed on his cigar.

"It's a terrible rout," sighed Sir Lucian. "I was sure my Queen had your Knight stymied." He reached for his cigar lighter, and then offered Dominick and Donato each a cigar.

"Cuban," he said. "Makes traveling across the pond worthwhile."

"Got these in Havana," La Bella Figura added.

"You were in Cuba?"

"No, Havana. It's a Brooklyn bar." He laughed and suddenly adopted a Brooklynese accent. "My name is Ernesto Cacciavolpe. I'm Brooklyn born and Neopolitan bred, like you Dominick, *paesan*."

"Why are you traveling to Naples?" Donato asked.

Sir Lucian explained. "He's keeping watch on the White King, the Italian dictator. The Black King, the Spanish dictator, is checked. You see, Mussolini and Franco rely on oil and money. Where these go, allegiances follow." He sighed, then continued.

"With the British presence in Gibraltar, we've got a toehold of land on Franco's very door step. Thus, he won't attempt an alliance with Hitler or Mussolini and will remain neutral."

Ernesto relit his cigar. "With British control of Gibraltar, Spain's hands are tied."

"And we control the entrance to the Mediterranean at the Pillars of Hercules," Sir Lucian said.

Dominick and Donato nodded. But they weren't interested in geopolitics.

"I'm glad your chess game is going well," Dominick said, "but we're looking for a murderer on board, one who killed both Juliet and Dr. Mahlberg."

The two men looked up in surprise. "I thought Juliet was a suicide. Dr. Mahlberg, you say, was also murdered? I thought he fell." Sir Lucian contemplated. "It seems we need better intelligence."

"May we go into your stateroom for a moment?" Donato asked Ernesto.

He opened the adjoining door, and the men walked into the next room. It was very opulent, even more so than Sir Lucian's, and almost twice as large.

"Courtesy of Il Duce," said Ernesto.

"May we see your accessories?" Donato asked.

The man opened his armoire, and pulled out a drawer. "They are all here. Tie clips, watches, rings, cufflinks, belts, etcetera."

Donato carefully examined the fashionable collection of the man's finest Egyptian cotton shirts and cuffs, the beautiful light merino wool and linen suits, the softest felt fedora hats and the brightly polished calf's leather shoes, and sighed. La Bella Figura was well-dressed indeed.

There were several items with *fascia* emblems, ties and tie clips and a scarf pin, but they didn't match the cufflink.

He held up the cufflink. "Have you ever seen this before?"

"No, I haven't. It's a beautiful cufflink, but it's marred by that *fascia* emblem."

"So you're not a fascist?"

"No, I'm your US Government attaché. My identity must remain secret. May I have your assurances?"

The men nodded.

"What will you do when you return to Italy?" Donato asked.

"Hope they don't discover who I really am. That would be the firing squad, and those Blackshirts don't simply give a single bullet to the back of the head. I'll do my best to make sure that doesn't happen."

Sir Lucian walked into the room and suggested they return to his stateroom for a drink. Once the men were seated in front of the chessboard, he opened a bottle of Chateau Margaux, while the attaché continued.

"So far, the fascists haven't joined Hitler, but they're authoritarians. As Sir Lucian explained, Franco is checked by the Brits —Mussolini won't have Spain's support in his Mediterranean empire building scheme. Where will he turn next? He'll need to form an alliance with Hitler. Mussolini and Fascists have no quarrel with the Jews, but if Mussolini forms an alliance with Hitler, that would change. In fact, we know from Dr. Malhberg that Hitler is about to adopt more anti-Jewish legislation with the racist Citizenship Law. Hate, strangely enough, garners power, and power is dangerous." He put the kings back on the board and moved chess pieces into position.

"After Mussolini invades Ethiopia, the dominoes will start falling. Hitler and Mussolini invade neighboring countries, like Czechoslovakia, Albania and Greece," he moved the kings forward, taking several pawns and knights. "Then Hitler aims to destroy Britain," he knocked down bishops. "Then Mussolini and Hitler will need Russian oil," and he knocked down the queens. "The US won't be neutral for long."

"So you were discussing politics on the balcony the night that Dr. Mahlberg was killed?"

"Yes, we were relaying information from Dr. Mahlberg about the new anti-Jewish law. He's part of Nazi medical research. We needed Dr. Mahlberg alive because he's a source of important information. We wouldn't have killed him, no matter how distasteful his views."

"And Juliet, I mean, Signorina Freda—did she play any role in this espionage game?" asked Dominick.

"Not that we know of," said Ernesto. "But we were watching her. She was very talented and beautiful, but she was a fascist and it was likely she would have led us to the head of the Nazi-Fascist organization."

"You mean as bait," said Dominick. The men shrugged.

Dominick and Donato accepted two Havana cigars, said good day, and left the Upper Deck staterooms.

They stopped on the Promenade Deck to watch the vast expanse of dark ocean as they lit their cigars. Dominick decided he could trust

Donato fully. It was time to mention that Chief Detective O'Malley had intelligence that the ship might be smuggling arms.

"We'll conduct a search below decks tomorrow," smiled Donato. "I'm looking forward to that."

"Well, so far, Cardinal Schlummer and Devil's Advocate are suspicious, but we can't prove they were involved in the doctor's death. I believe we can rule out Sir Lucian and La Bella Figura—they seem to be preoccupied with world affairs, and in any case, they needed Juliet and Dr. Mahlberg alive."

"Let's continue our interview with Lady Montague, Bella Arrabia, and Lord Capulet, Tomasso Confitura."

"These two families seem to be at war, not only about Freda and Alfredo, but something else," Dominick said. "We need to find out what that is."

They continued down the hall and knocked on a stateroom door on A Deck.

Lady Montague opened the door, looking displeased. She motioned them inside, dressed in an elegant satin dressing gown with ostrich feather collar. "You want to know why we were talking on the Promenade Deck?"

"Yes. Where's Lord Capulet? Hiding in the closet?" Dominick asked.

Lady Montague went to the adjoining door and knocked. Lord Capulet unlocked his side and then entered the state room.

"Signora Arrabia, Lady Montague, are you having an affair with Tomasso Confitura, Lord Capulet?" Donato asked.

She bristled. "Of course not. I can't stand him. He's not, how do you say, strong enough for me. He's not a fascist."

"I am a fascist. But I'm not like you."

"So what were you doing together on the Promenade Deck, before Dr. Mahlberg's death?"

"We just happened to both be outside for a stroll, and exchanged a few words."

"You were seen having a heated conversation, not just a few words. Twice in fact. Also in the hallway by the ship's painting."

"Oh, that Dr. Reva. She exaggerates."

"Nonetheless, you were seen twice together."

"Okay, we'd been trying to break up the engagement of our children, Freda and Alfredo, but as you know, the dear girl died. So we were showing remorse, blaming ourselves, asking whether we had something to do with Freda's suicide, if our efforts had made her kill herself."

"We now know she was murdered—poisoned."

"Oh my poor daughter," Lord Capulet sat on the sofa with his head in his hands.

"We had nothing to do with that," Lady Montague snapped.

"What about Dr. Mahlberg? Was he your physician on board the ship?"

"Yes, I was a patient of his," said Lord Capulet.

"What ailment did you have,"

"Nothing life threatening."

"And you, Signora Confitura?"

"A private matter."

"Can I see your cufflinks?" Dominick asked Lord Montague.

"Certainly," Lord Montague outstretched his arms, revealing his cuffs pinned with monogrammed silver cufflinks. Then he took Dominick and Donato through the adjoining door into his stateroom and opened a box on his dresser. "There, all my watches, rings, pins, my many medals, etcetera."

There were no *fascia* emblems on any jewelry, only on the medals. Nor were there any *fascia* cufflinks on his shirt or the shirts hanging in his armoire.

Dominick and Donato said goodbye and left the stateroom.

The two men walked down the hallway. Dominick remarked, "There's something going on between those two, but they aren't lovers."

"How can you tell?"

"There was no chemistry between the two, no sparks of electricity."

"Maybe they're old lovers who are now friends with adjoining cabins?"

"More likely enemies. They were withholding something from us."

"We should look at Dr. Mahlberg's files and find out what ailments they were being treated for," Donato said.

"Good idea. I'll ask Olivia, I mean Dr. Porter-Graves, to look when she's working." Dominick replied. "Cardinal Schlummer and that Devil's Advocate acted suspiciously, and the cufflink places one of them at the scene of Dr. Mahlberg's death."

"But they're priests. Surely they can't be murderers."

"It's odd there was only one Bible in the room. I don't believe that the cardinal misplaced his Holy book."

"That is suspicious."

"Lady Montague and Lord Capulet—they're not lovers, but perhaps they plotted together? But why kill Freda, his daughter? Why kill Dr. Mahlberg, their physician?"

Chapter 13 - Briscola

T he length of the First Class Veranda was lined with white clothed tables and chairs, with potted palm trees between them creating a screen for private conversations.

Seated at one of the longer card tables at the far end were the Capulets and Montagues, chatting amicably.

Maria and Antonio approached, intent on doing some sleuthing on the foursome.

The opera stars invited them to sit down and take an *aperitivo*, aperitif. They all spoke in their native Italian.

"We were just about to play *Briscola*. Won't you join us? We can play with three couples."

Lord Capulet shuffled a stack of cards drawn with swords (*spade*), cups (*coppe*), coins (*danari*), and clubs (*bastoni*). There were court cards, called "*vestite*" meaning dressed.

The deck had no 10's, 9's, or 8's. Oddly, Aces and 3's were the top scoring cards.

"I'll explain Briscola to you, as you've surely forgotten our national card game when you became American. Ace is the high card worth 11 points, then Three is worth 10 points, then *Re*, King is worth four points. The Horse,or *Cavallo* is three points, Jack or *Fante* is two points. All the rest of the cards are worthless, *Scarte frusc' e pigl' primmere*. Remember, worthless."

"There's no Queen?"

No, the Dama is at home having babies." Lord Capulet said, looking at Lady Capulet. "From her own husband."

"Mussolini's Battle for Births, we need 60 million pure blood Italians, or how are we going to run an empire?" laughed Lady Capulet.

"We need an army of soldiers—legions," opined Lord Montague. "Our role is to be the soldiers of culture."

"Maria, how did you become a soprano. I doubt you can even hit a high C," Lady Montague challenged.

The two divas glared at Maria.

Maria was taken aback by Lady Montague's strident tone, but she hit the note, saying "I can hit any C, as good as anyone else."

Antonio clenched his fists behind his back. Sleuthing with such a displeasing group of fascists required restraint.

"No, not like that, Maria," Lady Montague continued. "Opera is a force more powerful than life itself. It is the voice of Italy. Put some emotion into it. Again."

Maria wanted to improve her singing voice, so she repeated the High C. "There."

"Ha, your anger didn't work any better," Lady Montague taunted.

"No, Bella. Maria has a wonderful voice," said Lord Montague.

Turning to Maria, he added, "Our voices give glory to our country. Once you're back in Italy, you'll see how it's improved under Mussolini. You'll never return to that pile of grime, New York City."

"But surely," Lord Capulet interrupted, "New York is also a great economic city. One can see the potential —"

"It's our duty to bring America into the fold of Fascism," Lady Montague interjected, raising her arm in the Fascist salute. The other divas and dons mimicked her. Lord Capulet reluctantly raised his arm, too.

Maria wanted to gag, but she calmed that reflex. But she noticed that Antonio had risen his arm in the salute. She hoped he was joining them to spy on them.

"*Il Duce!*" said Lord Montague.

He pulled out a chair for Maria and then sat down himself. "Who's ready to play some cards?"

"Where's Alfredo?" Maria asked, to lighten the mood.

He's recuperating. He's very distraught to return to Naples without his beloved Juliet—my poor Freda," said Lady Capulet sadly.

"Truly a great loss to our troupe and to our country," said Lord Montague. "She had such a beautiful voice. A songbird."

"I don't know about that. She hit the high C's, but as for the lower notes—all bluster," Lady Montague countered and dealt the cards, three apiece.

The players picked up their hands. Maria noticed that they made strange lip curls, mouth twists, and other signals to their partner, depending on the trumps in their hands.

Lady Montague turned the top card face up. It was the Ace of Spades. Spades were then supposed to be the trump cards. But Lady Montague placed the Ace in her hand and claimed it as her own. She then turned over the next card. She didn't want to leave that one as a trump card, either, so she placed it at the bottom of the pack, and then finally settled for the third card, a four of cups.

"You can't choose the trump. That's cheating," Maria said.

"The dealer chooses as she likes, *come le piace.*"

"It's useless to play for points. Let's add some money," said Lord Capulet. All agreed and put $5 dollars each on the table.

The players played cards down.

"Don't you have any *vestiti*, court cards?" huffed Lady Montague to her husband.

He put down a baton Queen.

"No, you idiot. You need to put down a cup," Lady Montague said impatiently, picking up his baton and giving him a cup card.

"Cavallo, horse, of cups, that's three points" said Lord Capulet, placing his card over the others and taking the pile, as his partner gave him a peck on the cheek.

"But that's not fair," said Maria. "My Queen of cups was higher."

Lady Capulet gave her an icy stare.

"You Americans, you make laws about equality, but no one is truly equal. It is a farce. Has it gotten you anywhere, Maria and Antonio? You're lowly immigrants and you will never be allowed to access the corridors of power. Are you happier, richer? Do you have a better future in America than in Italy?

"No. You are in the dark ages, afraid of your own shadow. America is a country of gangsters and cowboys."

"Freedoms, civil liberties! You make these laws, then you flout them anyway. There's no equality in America. It's a lie," added Lady Montague.

"Mussolini—he takes care of everyone. Everyone has a role. Italian fascism is the only solution. It works for all."

"Everyone must subjugate themselves to the State," added Lord Montague.

"*By whatever means necessary*," added Lady Montague.

"There are tens of thousands of Americans who want to join us. Thousands in Brooklyn alone. Why? Because Mussolini brings order to the chaos," said Lady Capulet. "Americans are corrupt from such impurity."

"Italians, by contrast, are the *razza pura*, the pure race. We are descendants of the Romans," said Lord Montague.

"I believe in Rome, the Eternal Mother country..." The divas and dons recited their oath. "I believe in the genius of Mussolini, and in the resurrection of the Empire." The lords and ladies raised their arms in the fascist salute.

"Isn't that the Nazi salute?" asked Maria.

"No, he stole it from us—it's the *Saluto Romano*, the ancient Roman Salute."

"Remember our days in the Youth Guard?" said Lord Montague.

"Of course. The youths are legionaries, the adult soldiers become centurions," said Lord Capulet.

Maria started to laugh, believing this to be some childish game, but Antonio tapped her foot gently under the table. She then realized the divas and dons believed such nonsense, and their tirade might help Josephine's investigation.

As sickened as she was listening to them, she asked what they'd been doing in Brooklyn to promote their cause.

"By performing, we're demonstrating that Mussolini has many gifts to bring to the savage Americans," said Lady Capulet.

"To Mussolini," she raised her arm. The fascist divas and dons saluted in return.

"So you come to Italy because you believe in fascism?" Lord Montague asked Maria and Antonio.

"Yes, I'm interested," said Antonio. "Whatever can make us Italians strong again is fine by me."

"Who organized your cultural trip to Brooklyn?" asked Maria.

"The orders came from Mussolini himself," said Lady Montague proudly.

"You mean, you spoke to him personally?"

"No, of course not. He's a very busy man." said Lady Capulet.

"We must civilize your country in one, how do you say, fell swoop," said Lord Montague. "It takes violence to put down the insurrections. You must suspend civil liberties, like we've done in Italy."

"You can't do that in America."

"Why not? *Me ne frego!* I don't give a darn. Mussolini's Blackshirts kill anyone who opposes him. He gets rid of undesirables in society."

"And he restores order to the home. Women should be keepers of the hearth," said Lady Montague. "Look at that doctor, Josephine Reva. She's taken a man's job."

"And not produced a single child," added Lady Capulet. "How many babies did you produce, Maria?"

"Uh, three."

"Three is a good start."

Lord Montague exclaimed and put down a five of clubs. He took the pile of cards.

"But..." Maria began. The five was worthless and didn't beat her *Fante,* Jack. "That's my trump."

"So? Why can't I have it?"

Maria started to protest, but Antonio tapped her under the table. He covered for her. "Of course, take it. Please continue."

"What about the people who live in America, the immigrants who came for work or a better life?" Maria asked.

"Mussolini's OVRA will take charge and send them all to Lipari or Ponza prison camps," said Lady Capulet.

"Castor oil poison," added Lady Montague. "That's my favorite. It's a quick but terrible death."

"How horrid!" Maria exclaimed.

"Horrid is that president of yours."

"Why don't you like FDR?" Antonio asked.

"Roosevelt can't compare to our *Il Duce*, Mussolini."

"He can't even goose step," the divas and dons laughed.

Antonio responded, paraphrasing FDR, that it was amazing what some middle-aged men physically can do when driven to extremes. Maria and Antonio laughed at the joke. But the opera stars were not amused.

"The US is neutral," Antonio said, "and we don't want to be involved in any European war ever again."

The opera stars smiled. "Germany is re-arming, and the Western countries need the Stressa Front more than they care about Ethiopia," said Lord Montague. "They will not stop us. Italy will become an empire after we invade Ethiopia and join it with Italian Libya.

"We failed last time, but we'll take it now. We'll control Eastern Africa and the Mediterranean, like our great emperors of long ago." The Lords and Ladies gave the Roman Salute again.

Lord Montague shuffled and cut the cards, then dealt three apiece.

"What's politics got to do with Juliet's death?" Antonio whispered to Maria.

"They're all fascists, including Juliet. So who would have wanted her dead?"

Lady Capulet looked at the gold watch pinned to her blouse. "We've been playing for over an hour. You must all be tired and hungry. We need a *toccasano*, a pick-me-up." She called for a porter to bring some afternoon snacks and drinks.

"Let's play *Rais,*" she announced. "Only the King can speak—it's a rule."

"What can he say?" Maria warily asked.

"He can ask if you've got any *Lisci*, useless cards worth zero points."

"But that's still cheating," sighed Maria.

"No, that's power. A leader, like Mussolini and *la Partita fascista*, the Fascist Party," said Lord Montague.

"The *Rais* is a corporatist. Corporatists make things better for all —they always have everyone's interests at heart," added Lady Montague.

"So, can the *Rais* ask if you have any *Briscoline* low trumps like 2 to 6's?" asked Antonio.

"Yes, and he can ask if you have any *Vestite* high trumps like the court cards, too," said Lord Montague.

"And the *Rais* can ask about *Carichi*—the highest point cards, an Ace or a 3 of any non-trump suit," added Lady Capulet.

"But that's everything!" said Maria. "Is there anything the *Rais* can't do?"

"The *Rais* can also order his partner what to play, too: a trump, a *Caricho, Liscio* or lead with no trump."

Maria sighed. "I don't see how this is any fun at all."

"Let's mix up the couples," Lady Montague announced. "That'll be even more fun. Tomasso, Gisella's husband, will play with Maria, and my husband, Salvatore, will play with Gisella, and myself with Antonio."

They exchanged their seats around the table. The porter returned and laid a plate of sweet cakes on the table, and a large fruit bowl of wild berries.

Another porter offered a tray of liqueurs to the players. Each chose their own glass.

At that moment, Isabella Schiavone and Fernando Delitto sashayed over.

"Is this my favorite plum liquor?" Fernando asked, taking one of the liqueur glasses off the tray and sniffing it.

The porter nodded and went to fetch two more glasses from the side table.

Lord Capulet reached forward hungrily. Lady Capulet slapped his hand. "*Scarte frusc' e pigl' primmere.* Some cards, like some berries, have value, but the blue berries are *pigli*—no value." She held out the fruit bow. "The blackest berries are sweetest."

She explained to Maria and Antonio, "He's diabetic."

"What are you playing at," Isabella asked, pointing to the cards. She took a handful of berries from the bowl, and a glass of liqueur.

"It's a new Stressa Front," laughed Lord Capulet, referring to Maria and Antonio, "now we're joining with the Americans."

He raised his glass to the couple, and the merry group laughed, then toasted and sipped their liqueurs.

"We're opposing Hitler's plan," he continued. "But we only need some breathing room until we can dominate Eastern Africa and the Mediterranean."

"Americans are still neutral," Isabella gestured towards Maria and Antonio. "Fools."

"The Americans won't stop Mussolini's invasion of Ethiopia. They'll only enact sanctions to protest it. These, of course, will be useless because they won't include oil, coal or gas."

"Sanctions will just be *una tirata d'orecchi*," Lady Montague added. "How do you Americans say that? A pull of the ear?"

"A slap on the wrist," said Antonio.

"Who slaps a wrist?" Lady Montague asked.

"How silly! Americans!" Isabella added.

"Italians have great language, culture, fashion, and, of course, opera," Lord Montague boasted. "Fascists are proud of what we've accomplished."

"I don't think Fascism will play very well in Brooklyn," said Maria.

"Oh, but it does," said Lady Capulet.

"What do you mean?"

"Before the opera, we attended fascist meetings— thousands of Brooklynites were there. They love Mussolini."

"We didn't know about it, or we would've gone, too," said Antonio, tapping Maria's foot under the table. "How do we find out about these meetings."

"The Brooklyn Fascist Society."

"How do we contact them? Is there a leader?"

"The leader is in Italy, a man of great persuasion."

"Who's that?"

"His identity is secret. We only received telegrams from Rome, which were to be destroyed after reading," said Lord Montague. "Now let's play. Shall we say double bets?"

Antonio looked worried. Who was sending telegrams to Brooklynites from the Italian Fascist government? He'd be sure to tell Dominick not only that, but how much he was losing in this crooked game. Would he be reimbursed by the Brooklyn PD?

SOLIS MUNDI

Chapter 14 - Storm

A fierce storm raged that evening, and most of the passengers remained in their cabins. The large waves beat against the ships's bow, and rain lashed the decks.

The ship was in the messy chop of the eastern Atlantic Ocean. Dominick gripped the side rails as he stood on the bridge, peering out the rain-spattered glass into the eye of the storm.

Donato clung to the steering wheel, piloting the ship through the tempest. The muscles on his arms tensed as each wave crashed against the ship. He wiped some sweat from his brow.

"Mind if I have a go?" asked Dominick. "I'd love to drive her."

"Sure, just for a minute. Ride the crests, and then steer her at an angle like this, to surf down the wave," Donato put his hand over Dominick's to guide him as the two gripped the wheel. "Then plow across the trough and back up the next crest."

Dominick felt the turbulence.

"She's not as responsive as my motor car," he said, reluctantly, letting Donato take back the wheel.

"These high winds are westerlies," Donato said. "They're coming from behind us and pushing us faster along. We'll surely break the record for our crossing."

"When will we arrive in Gibraltar?"

"If the winds keep up, we'll be there by first light."

Dominick looked at the newly arrived wireless telegram from Chief Detective O'Malley asking for an update, and reminding him to check for contraband arms.

Donato called over several officers to take the wheel and plotted the course. "I'll relieve you at midnight." He turned to Dominick. "Dinner?"

The two walked towards the door.

"Donato,Italy is fast becoming a belligerent nation. Would now be a good time to search the ship?"

Donato nodded. "Shall we check the engine room first?"

The pair set off below decks.

* * *

Josephine, Saltzie, Maria and Antonio had reconvened in Saltzie's stateroom to plan their next steps.

Josephine took another *Cocculus indicus* pill from one of the vials in her traveling homeopathic remedy case. She dissolved it in few tablespoons of water from the pitcher, which she'd poured into a glass.

Maria was laying and moaning on the sofa.

Josephine handed Maria the remedy, and Maria gratefully swallowed it.

"That should help with the seasickness," Josephine said. "How are you in this rough weather, Saltzie and Antonio?"

"We're fine," Saltzie said. "I'm a sailor and Antonio has his sea legs."

"That's good. Well, what's our plan? There are two deaths, Juliet's and Dr. Mahlberg's, both from Belladonna. They must be connected somehow."

"We learned that the opera stars made contact with a Brooklyn Fascist group. It's run by someone in Mussolini's government, but we don't know who that is," said Antonio.

"Let's look at the jar test." Josephine said. "Maybe there's another clue." She ventured out on the balcony of the swaying boat, trying to hold herself steady and keeping her eyes on the horizon line. She pulled the jar from its ring, and brought it back inside.

"I wish this boat would stop rocking," she said, as she tried to hold the jar steady.

"Technically, it's the sea that's rocking," laughed Saltzie. "We sailors just think of it as bumps in the road."

"I wish te road was not so bumpy," moaned Maria.

Josephine was staring at the jar.

"That's odd," she said. "The solids are floating. Usually a solid mass is heavier than water. Heavy plant matter would sink to the bottom."

"What is it, then?" Antonio asked.

Saltzie came over. "The color is strange. Greeny-blue. Here, let me open it."

He opened the jar and a small green cloud escaped. Saltzie's nose was right there and he got a strong whiff of it. "Ugh, that's odious." He suddenly fell onto the chair. "Like rotten eggs. I'm dizzy," he said and swooned.

"Saltzie, are you okay," Josephine ran over to him. "He's fainted." She took the pitcher of water and poured it over his face. "Saltzie, please, wake up." She put her hand to his forehead.

The gas from the jar filled the air, and the others gagged.

"Quick, Antonio, open the balcony door and porthole window," Josephine commanded.

Antonio complied and fresh sea air filled the stateroom. Saltzie sputtered.

"Whew!" said Maria.

"Yes, that was close," said Antonio. "We'd all have been a goner."

Saltzie sat up and held his head, moaning. "Whatever that gas was, it was strong."

"Saltzie, that smell! Juliet's vomit reeked of that same smell," Josephine exclaimed.

"Yes, you're right. It was horrible."

"And Dr. Mahlberg's stomach contents had a similar smell," she continued. "I think they were poisoned by this same blue-green matter."

"What on earth is it? A solid or a gas? I've never been knocked off my socks like that before."

"Yes, it was like you got sucker punched," said Antonio.

"I don't know what it is," said Josephine. "But I'll find out." She set to work reconfiguring the lab to test the matter.

Several hours passed, and she was no closer to discovering what the matter could be. "The gas is gone, and I don't have any way to test that."

"Let's take a break," Saltzie said. "It's nearly dinner time."

The group left to get dressed in formal wear for the evening. Josephine walked down the great hallway to her cabin.

The papier-maché wall painting showed the *SS Rex* pulled along on its wire all the way to the coast of Spain, and approaching the Pillars of Hercules. *Oh dear*, she thought, *tomorrow we'll arrive in Gibraltar. I'm no closer to solving this case than before we left!*

Josephine found her own invitation to the Captain's table slid under her stateroom door. This time, the invitation specified "white tie", and it was addressed to "Dr. Josephine Reva +1 guest." She couldn't wait to boast about it to Saltzie. He could be her "plus one guest" this time, and for the ship's formal dinner, no less.

Having only the same evening dress, the beautiful one sewn by Maria with its intricate handiwork, she decided to wear it again and pair it with a silk crocheted jacket. *Maybe that dreadful Isabella won't notice.*

Someone knocked at the cabin door. It was the friendly young porter again.

"Hello Dr. Reva," he said. "I have orders to bring you this, from Isabella Schiavone." He held out a wardrobe dress hanger with a dress wrapped in tissue paper. He excitedly waited for her to unwrap it.

It was a silk halter dress with a deeply plunging neckline, in shades of phosphorescent ocean greens and blues. The frothy skirt was emblazoned with a giant squid dripping ink.

"Wow, thanks," said Josephine, turning the dress around. "But it's missing the back."

"Yeah, it sure shows a lot of skin," said the porter, letting out a wolf whistle. "You'll look very sexy in that. I've got something to tell the boys back in Brooklyn."

"Oh, dear," replied Josephine, taking the dress. "Please tell Maria to come help me."

* * *

At a quarter to eight, Saltzie straightened his bow tie, and knocked at Josephine's door.

Maria opened it. "She's notta ready. We're still trying to piece together her dress."

"Isabella forgot to send the back of it," called Josephine. She came forward and stood embarrassed before Saltzie, adjusting the front halter, which barely covered her breasts. She then turned to show that the rear of the dress had only a band just across her butt, showing off her naked back and legs.

"Wowee! I'm not exactly an expert in fashion," Saltzie began, "but I like it!"

"I can't go out looking like this."

"Here, put on my jacket, that'll cover you. Now let's go get the missing pieces of this dress from Isabella."

Josephine, Maria and Saltzie stumbled down the rocking hallway, passing the ship's papier-maché painting. The model of the *SS Rex* was now hanging off of its wire, capsized.

They found Isabella's stateroom and knocked. There was no answer. "Do you think she's already gone to dinner?"

"Itsa too early for her," said Maria. "She likes to make a grand entrance."

"Signora Schiavone?" Saltzie called.

Josephine put her ear to the door. "I hear her. She sounds sick."

"Porter, quick!" Saltzie called to a porter on his rounds. "Please open this door immediately." The porter used his pass key.

They group entered to find Isabella Schiavone gurgling in agony, and grabbing her throat. She was sputtering and choking.

"Quickly, Porter, please go get my medical kit," Josephine said. "Maria, we need plenty of salt and a glass of water."

Josephine and Saltzie set about examining Isabella.

"She's got the same symptoms as Juliet," exclaimed Josephine. "She's been poisoned!"

"Do you think it's that same Belladonna poison?"

"I think so, but there's no smell like rotten eggs this time."

Fernando Delitto, Cardinal Schlummer and the Devil's Advocate entered from their neighboring cabins, hearing the commotion.

"Poison?" the cardinal asked. "Are we in any danger?

"Are we all going to die?" Fernando asked. "I can't die now, not before my next show."

"Let's help her vomit," said Josephine, pouring some salty water into Isabella's mouth.

The fashionista vomited profusely, but it didn't seem to help her. She continued gurgling, flopped limply on the ground, her mouth gaping open, and then went still.

"Just like a fish," said Fernando.

Cardinal Schlummer and the Devil's Advocate began murmuring Last Rites.

Chapter 15 - Gibraltar

The *SS Rex* sounded its horn, and the great ship thrust its engines into reverse to maneuver alongside the concrete wharf. Deck hands threw thick coiled ropes onto the piers, and pulled the ship to rest calmly against the posts.

They then lowered the gangplanks for passengers to depart into the sunny Mediterranean city.

Josephine stood on the lower Promenade Deck, thinking how soon they would be in Fascist Italy. *The killer must know that he or she is almost home free. So why kill Dr. Mahlberg and Isabella Schiavone, too?*

The massive Rock of Gibraltar loomed overhead, dominating the landscape. Josephine had never seen a rock so huge, nor a cliff so high, falling sharply to the crystal blue Mediterranean Sea, which crashed against its base.

Her gaze returned to the dock, where the body bags of Juliet, Dr. Mahlberg and Isabella Schiavone were being unloaded into waiting funeral vans.

"They'll be transported to their home countries," said Sir Lucian, who came to join Josephine at the railing, "for proper burials. I'm glad the captain didn't dispose of the bodies at sea." He looked pensive, then continued.

"Well, it's back to work, up there," he pointed to a large villa above the harbor, with its balcony overlooking the Mediterranean. "You must come visit if you're ever back to Gibraltar. I cultivate the sweetest oranges and finest lemons in all the colony."

"That's a very kind offer, Sir Lucian. But I'm so busy with my medical practice, I doubt I'll ever have the opportunity to visitEurope again."

"I understand. Then please remember me from time to time over the coming years, when things become grave on this side of the Atlantic."

"You think there'll be another war so soon?"

"With Hitler's Reich Citizenship Laws and Mussolini's upcoming invasion of Abyssinia, things are headed in that direction. I'll do my utmost to make sure Franco stays neutral. The Royal Navy will guard these straits, and no German U-Boat or naval cruiser will pass through the Pillars of Hercules without us knowing."

"An English gentleman's retirement on the sunny coast, but while I'm gardening, I'll be looking to entrap another Dr. Mahlberg."

He tipped his top hat. "Dr. Reva, I wish you good luck in catching the Fascist murderer. I'm very glad we're on the same side of right and wrong—you with your poisons, and me with my citruses."

He walked jauntily down the gangplank, tapping his walking stick.

* * *

Dominick was swinging his body higher on the trapeze exercise bars on the Sports Promenade Deck. *What a view!* he thought, as he soared above the parallel bars. The clean sea air filled his lungs, and inspired by the massive Rock of Gibraltar panorama, he swung even higher. He arched his back and left the bars with a flying mid-air somersault and flipped to the mat below, landing on his feet.

Olivia was waiting and held out a towel for him. "Impressive," she said with a smile. "I mean our trapeze act last night."

He placed his arms on her hips, and holding her steady, lifted her tall frame high in the air above him. "How about more exercise tonight?"

She nodded and smiled. "After my mother retires, I'll come meet you in your stateroom."

Dominick said a cheery goodbye, then headed for the Bridge.

He climbed the stairs two at a time, feeling exceptionally chipper.

But he knew he had serious business with Donato.

"We've arrived to Gibraltar 12 hours ahead of schedule!" exclaimed Donato jubilantly, as Dominick entered the Bridge. He followed along as Dominick went to check for any telegraphs. "This bodes well for my Blue Riband—it's coming back to me! This ship is truly the fastest—I've never seen her engines so finely tuned."

"Yes, they did look amazing yesterday. Maybe we should take another look below decks? You can explain to me again how they work."

Donato nodded eagerly, and led the way out the door to the main deck. They stopped at the railing to smoke a cigarette and look out over the Rock of Gibraltar.

"Fabulous, isn't it?"

"What?" asked Dominick.

"That giant rock, hard as you like."

"I know what you mean," said Dominick, and the two laughed. "Are the waters we're entering in the Mediterranean tonight controlled by Gibraltar?"

"No. Territorial waters only extend so far, about ten to twelve miles or so from the coastline. Then there are areas with fishing rights, and then ecologically protected areas. But that only accounts for a small fraction of the Mediterranean Sea. A great deal of it is still considered 'the high seas'."

"You mean that no country controls it?"

"Yes. Look at this map." Donato pulled out a folded survey on the Mediterranean from his pocket. "Here's Gibraltar in English waters, and there's the island of Mallorca in Spanish waters. When we sail into this area here," he pointed to an area between the two, "we'll be far enough away from both, and far from the Spanish coast."

"That's considered the 'high seas'?"

"Yes."

"Why don't countries claim all the waters in the Med?"

"They certainly fight about it. But the more waters they claim, the more they must spend money to protect fish stocks, conserve it from pollution, and defend their territory from attack. I suppose it's too expensive and not worth the trouble."

"I see, so there's a lot of unclaimed water."

"Yes, most of our voyage in the Med will be on the high seas," he laughed. "We'll be the captains of our own destinies. Just like the Barbary pirates! We can do whatever we like—drink, gamble, buy or sell anything! The waters are calmer and we can have a grand time. And Captain Bevilacqua does know how to throw a good party."

They descended below decks to the engine room. Donato was in his element, explaining how the steam operation worked, and pointing to a lot of switches and levers, and encouraging Dominick to read the dials.

"I was an ambulance mechanic in the Great War," Dominick said. "This machinery is top of the line."

When Donato's back was turned, Dominick casually dropped a wrench down one of the saline water turbines.

***

Saltzie was leaning against the railing on the Upper Promenade, and a porter brought him an up-to-date newspaper. But he was dismayed to read the latest headline:

"Nazi Germany announces two new laws: The Law for the Protection of German Blood and German Honor and the Reich Citizenship Law. The first law prohibits the marriage of non-Jews with Jews..."

Saltzie threw down the newspaper in disgust. *Thankfully, we're not traveling to Germany*, he thought, *but if we did live there, Josephine and I would no longer be allowed to marry. How absurd!*

As he walked back through First Class to his stateroom, he passed a well-heeled couple walking the other way.

"Dirty Jew," they said in a hateful tone of voice.

Saltzie stopped in shock. *What is the world coming to?*

He took out his key and unlocked his stateroom door.

At sunset, the *SS Rex* eased out of Gibraltar's harbor, pushing her great weight steadily against the currents. After fighting the Straits, she slipped quietly into the international waters of the Mediterranean Sea.

Chapter 16 - Mediterranean Currents

At dinner that evening, Saltzie was sullen, and glad he was no longer invited to sit at the Captain's Table.

Josephine, on the other hand, was becoming more outgoing. She whistled as Maria and Antonio went up onstage to entertain the other passengers.

The Lords and Ladies Capulet and Montague applauded, encouraging the amateurs to sing.

Maria and Antonio began with an Irving Berlin song from the latest movie, *Top Hat*. They sang to the happy tune "Cheek to Cheek", as passengers filled the dance floor.

Next they called Josephine to come up onstage.

"No, no. I'm really not that good," she protested.

"Yes, you are," they said.

The Italian divas and dons added that Italians have a natural singing voice. "Go on!" Lord Montague said. "Sing something American!"

The three of them, Maria, Antonio and Josephine, conferred and then sang "The Lullaby of Broadway," to raucous applause.

They huddled to decide on their next number.

Maria announced to the crowd that they would change the tempo, and she motioned to a waiter to dim the lights.

A spotlight found Antonio. With his deep baritone, he broke into the song "Summertime" from the hit musical Porgy and Bess.

It was an outstanding rendition, but the audience only gave scattered applause.

Josephine, Maria and Antonio sat back down, as the group of opera divas and dons got up to take the stage.

"Listen and learn, amateurs," Lady Montague sneered at Josephine as she passed.

The orchestra changed to an upbeat drumming tempo, and the divas and dons began to sing an energetic marching song.

The crowd of passengers went wild, clapping or tapping on the tables to the beat:

> *Oh, beautiful Black Abyssinian girl*
> *We've come to save you*
> *The Blackshirts will liberate you—*
> *Look! See our flag coming across the sea,*
> *waving for you, waving for you*
> *Your hour of freedom is near*
> *The only slavery is—*
> *we are slaves to you*
> *All for love and freedom!*

Josephine was disgusted. "They're about to conquer a sovereign country and commit genocide."

"No," said Delitto, "Italians are going to liberate the Ethiopians from themselves, from their slavery. The women will become free. The people will become cultured. If only we Spanish would join them."

Josephine turned away, and whispered to Saltzie.

"Somehow these fascists believe that they are saving the Abyssinian woman from.... from what? By killing all the men in the war? By destroying their country?"

"It's vile," agreed Saltzie, looking very glum.

The orchestra then played "Isle of Capri" and passengers happily went onto the dance floor for a tango foxtrot.

"Let's go outside," Josephine said. "I can't be around this."

"I'd say let's go back to my stateroom," said Saltzie. "But we're on a ship in the middle of what will soon be a war zone, and heading to a country of crazy fascists about to commit rape and genocide on poor Ethiopians. I'm not in the mood."

They walked outside and down the stairs to the Promenade Deck to be closer to the churning ocean, and take in the distant silhouette of the Mediterranean coastline. They stopped at the railing.

"How can this be so beautiful, when all is going to hell?"

"We've not found Juliet's murderer, and the killer has struck again," Josephine said. "The Nazi Dr. Mahlberg, and Isabella Schiavone, a fascist fashionista. What's the connection?"

Dominick, Olivia, Maria and Antonio joined them.

"We've gotta come up wit' a plan," said Maria. "We're almost to Nizza and Genova. Then Napoli, and itsa all over."

"What did you see during the card game?"

"They're fascists, that's for sure," Antonio said. "Isabella and Fernando did come over to join us. Isabella took some of the fruit and drink. But everybody took from the same bowl. The waiter handed out the glasses of liqueur, and they were all poured from the same decanter."

"Olivia, did you see anything in Dr. Mahlberg's files?" Dominick asked.

"Nothing really. Lady Capulet has a breast growth, and Lord Capulet has a low sperm count. That's kind of a private matter."

Henrietta came over. "Have you caught the murderer yet? Three fascist murders! This is exciting."

"No, I need more time," replied Josephine.

The ship's engines suddenly ground to a halt.

"What's that noise? What's happened?" asked Josephine.

"We're stopping," said Saltzie. "It sounds like something's broken with the engines."

"Don't worry," said Dominick. "I threw a wrench in the turbines. It won't harm anything, and should buy us another day."

Saltzie slapped Dominick on the back. The others praised him.

"Thank you, Dominick," said Josephine. "I know I can always count on you."

"Let's all go to bed," Dominick said. "We'll have plenty of time tomorrow to work this out. We're now back again on the high seas. There's still time to solve this case, we can turn the guilty party over to Donato."

"I can't wait to watch the action. But I'm very tired," said Henrietta, yawning. "Come Olivia, say goodnight and let's go back to our stateroom."

Olivia gave a wink to Dominick, which Josephine noticed.

Dominick smiled and excused himself. Maria and Antonio also retired, walking back to their stateroom, linking arms and smooching.

Josephine and Saltzie were left standing alone. Saltzie was still in a gloomy mood. Josephine tried to cheer him up by telling him some doctor jokes.

"Have you heard the one where the Patient says:

Who thumps my rump and thumps my chest,

pokes and pinches me with zest,

then says go home and get some rest?

My Doctor!"

But Saltzie was unenthused.

As they walked towards a deserted area of the deck, they heard someone praying. "Mother Cabrini, help me! I didn't mean—"

Josephine and Saltzie saw a figure climbing over the railing.

"Hey, wait! Don't jump," Saltzie called. They rushed over in the dark.

Suddenly, Josephine felt a strong push on her back, and she felt herself being lifted in the air, dangling over the ship's railing. Time seemed suspended. She could see nothing but the crush of the waves below.

I can't swim! She imagined herself thrown head first into the cold, dark churning waters, sinking ever lower. Was drowning to be her end?

She felt a tug, then her attacker released her, and she was falling, light as a feather in the air. But the skirt of her dress caught on the railing latch, and she was suspended above the ocean. Her hands found a bar of the metal railing, and she held on for dear life.

"Help!" she cried. "I'm over here."

There were sounds of a scuffle, and some muffled cries.

Strong hands began pulling her upwards. She felt one pair of hands, then another.

"Let go of her, Dominick," Saltzie was emphatic. "I've got you, Josephine."

"You couldn't even land a punch on her attacker," said Dominick. "Let me pull her up. My muscles are stronger, buddy."

"No need, buddy. I said I've got her."

"You're going to drop me!" Josephine gripped the top railing and swung her leg over it. She hauled herself up

"While you two are fighting, the killer is getting away!" She pointed to a dark shadow running off. "Don't just stand there, go after him!"

Dominick and Saltzie ran down the deck in hot pursuit.

Josephine stood on the Promenade Deck and exhaled.

She heard a creak by the life preserver station, and cautiously went over to it.

The area was dimly lit by a blue bulb, but it was casting an odd-shaped shadow. She crept up slowly, took one end of the life preserver rope, and circled the station.

She quickly pulled the rope tight, then ran around the life preserver station a second time.

"Aargh," a man's voice cried. She grabbed one of the preserver's wooden rods, and stuck it to twist the rope as tightly as possible, the way she tightened a tourniquet. Then she tied the rope off in a square knot.

Her attacker was now bound.

Dominick and Saltzie came racing around the deck to find a dark figure tied up with rope to the life preserver station. Saltzie flicked his lighter on.

"Father Della Pietra!" said Josephine. "Why did you try to kill me? Why did you kill Juliet? Because she was a fascist?"

"No!"

"And why kill Dr. Mahlberg? Because he was a Nazi?"

"No!"

"You were at the opera when Juliet died," said Saltzie. "And I found one of your cufflinks where Dr. Mahlberg was pushed overboard."

"But why kill Isabella Schiavone? She was just a silly fashion designer," asked Josephine.

"She was a fascist, too," added Saltzie.

"I didn't kill anyone," protested the Devil's Advocate, as Dominick pulled the ship's alarm bell. He took the excess rope and tied the Devil's Advocate's wrists behind his back roughly.

"Are you really a priest, or a thug?" asked Dominick.

"Just because I don't believe in miracles, doesn't mean I killed anyone."

"Well someone just tried to kill Josephine. If it wasn't you, then who was it?"

"Who tried to push Josephine overboard?" Saltzie asked. "What do you know?"

"I have nothing more to say. Arrest me if you must." Father Della Pietra hung his head low.

Donato and several officers came running. The Devil's Advocate was taken into custody, and marched to the ship's brig.

Chapter 17 - Dead in the Water

The next morning, news of the capture of Father Della Pietra was the talk at the breakfast buffet. Passengers were jubilant and relieved that the murderer was under guard, and many congratulated Josephine, Dominick and Saltzie.

"Youre' so brave, Josephine, tying up that wayward priest," said Henrietta. "You should be proud, but you look troubled."

"There's something that isn't adding up. I don't see the connection between Juliet, I mean Freda, Dr. Mahlberg, Isabella Schiavone and the Devil's Advocate. Why would the Devil's Advocate kill them?"

"Well, underneath their talented lives, those fascists and that Nazi were very bad people. A priest can't abide evil. And you said Father Della Pietra was about to jump overboard. Maybe his conscience couldn't excuse what he'd done."

"Maybe," replied Josephine. "But why would he try to kill me? I'm not a fascist."

Captain Bevilacqua made an announcement over the ship's loudspeaker:

"In celebration of our gallant crew and passengers, who apprehended a criminal aboard our ship, we are now back in safe hands. But due to unforeseen mechanical difficulties, we will remain drifting, but with anchors dropped, until repairs are made.

We assure you that we will be underway soon. In the meantime, please head up to our Sports Deck, where we will be hosting a full schedule of games and competitions for your enjoyment."

"I see you're prepared, as always," Henrietta pointed to Josephine's medical bag.

"Yes, when I hear sports competition, I think injuries." Josephine laughed. "Let's hope nothing else happens."

Saltzie ambled over and greeted Josephine and Mrs. Porter-Graves. "I signed up for the fencing tournament," he said. "Come and cheer me on, Joe and Henrietta, please!"

"I'd love to," said Henrietta. "There's Olivia talking with Dominick. We'll see you there."

"I hear Dominick is in the competition, and Romeo, and Lord Capulet, too" said Josephine, "so you'll have your work cut out for you."

"I can easily take them all on," boasted Saltzie, flashing his sword. "Shall we?"

He carried her medical bag for her. She took his arm and they walked up the stairs to the Sports Promenade.

The fencing competition got underway. Saltzie expertly parried and thrusted, and made it to the semi-finals. The remaining fencers were Dominick, Lord Capulet, and Romeo.

Saltzie drew Lord Capulet.

"Epee or foil?" Saltzie offered. "Saber is too fast, I'd guess."

"Foil," replied Lord Capulet. "I think you'd have the advantage of me with an epee or a saber. I'm not as strong as I once was in my youth."

On the other side of the field, Dominick and Romeo stretched and flexed their muscles while waiting for their turn.

Josephine watched as Saltzie's match was played first.

Saltzie lunged and easily scored a point on Lord Capulet's torso. "Touché!"

"I admit I haven't been practicing. The younger tenors get all the roles with any fencing," lamented Lord Capulet.

"I need some fight from you, so I can look good in front of my gal," Saltzie whispered, thrusting Lord Capulet backward. "Come on, then!'

They circled each other again, and Saltzie landed another touch to Lord Capulet's vest. "Look," he whispered, "I'll lead, you parry, then you can score a touch on me. Make it look convincing."

The two circled a few more times, and Saltzie faltered and fell to the ground dramatically. The crowd gasped. Lord Capulet landed the touch.

Saltzie turned to Josephine and she cheered to encourage him. "Get up, Saltzie!"

Saltzie's expert footwork let him easily dominate Lord Capulet and push him off the mat. Then he made his next assaults, and with several furious lunges, he touched Lord Capulet's vest. Lord Capulet appeared to be winded. He was breathing heavily and sank to his knees. He conceded. Lady Capulet rushed over to help him get up.

"Victory!" Saltzie shouted as he raised his foil and looked at Josephine. She smiled, whistled and applauded.

Next up were Dominick and Romeo. They'd chosen the heavier epees.

Romeo attacked off the mark, showing he was aggressive and well-trained from his performances. But Dominick countered ably, and his strategy seemed to be to play defense. He waited for his moment, and found a hole in Romeo's offensive and struck, hitting Romeo's thigh. Dominick received the point.

Josephine cheered. Saltzie harrumphed.

Dominick next went on the attack, wielding the epee like a baseball bat. He raised it high, preparing to swing it down on Romeo's head. But Romeo was easily able to go underneath and land his epee on Dominick's chest for the point.

Olivia booed.

The two men circled each other.

Dominick was battling for any advantage against a fierce onslaught of aggressive attacks. Romeo pushed Dominick backward to the edge of the mat. Dominick managed to hold him off, and Josephine thought he was using his earlier strategy, waiting to find a hole in the onslaught, but he stumbled in his footwork.

Romeo, sensing blood, came in for the kill, but he suddenly stopped. Dropping his sword, he tore at his mask. He pulled it off and was red in the face. He was gagging and choking.

Josephine and Saltzie rushed over and examined Romeo. "It's a good thing I brought my medical bag. Romeo might be having a seizure or —"

"Or he might be poisoned."

The two doctors worked diligently over Romeo. After using a stomach pump and gastric lavage with mustard, they arranged

Josephine's breathing apparatus with bellows. Romeo sputtered, and then began breathing deeply on his own.

Josephine and Saltzie had managed to stabilize his condition.

They wiped their brows.

"His symptoms were similar to Juliet's," said Josephine.

"But this time, we were quicker and knew what to expect."

"Yes, it does seem like Belladonna. But there's that strange odor again."

"It's that rotten egg smell that caused me to pass out in my stateroom."

"Yes, from the solid contents of Juliet's poison bottle."

"What do you think it is?"

"I don't know. I've never smelled anything like it before."

The opera's nurse came running over. "Please Dr. Reva, Dr. Saltzman, you've got to come help Friar Lawrence. He's not well."

Josephine and Saltzie rushed over to the pool area, where the friar was sprawled on a deck chair.

"He was drinking a cocktail," the nurse said, holding up a glass with a paper umbrella. "And the next thing I knew, he'd fainted."

Josephine and Saltzie examined Friar Lawrence. They went to work and set up another stomach pump and gastric lavage. The friar coughed up his drink, then seemed to be feeling better.

"Well, one thing for sure," said Saltzie. "Father Della Pietra had nothing to do with these latest crimes. He was in the ship's brig."

Josephine wondered—*could there be two killers?*

She decided to visit the Devil's Advocate in the ship's hold that evening after dinner. Donato sent an officer to accompany her below decks.

The cells were dark, dank and gloomy. The priest was kneeling and in deep prayer. Josephine waited patiently until he crossed himself, then spoke.

"Please tell me what you know, Father. There have been more poisoning attempts—Romeo and Friar Lawrence were taken ill. You must, therefore, be innocent. But who killed Juliet, Dr. Mahlberg and Isabella Schiavone? Who tried to kill Romeo, the friar and me? Is anyone else in any danger?"

The Devil's Advocate only replied: "Canon 983.1 of the Code of Canon Law, the Catechism, states that it is a crime for a confessor in any way to betray a penitent by word or in any other manner or for any reason. A priest cannot break the seal of the confessional to save his own life, to protect his good name, to refute a false accusation, to save the life of another, to aid the course of justice, or to avert a public calamity.

I'm sorry, but I can't help you, Dr. Reva."

He bent his head and continued to pray.

As Josephine returned to the upper deck, the ship's engines roared back to life. She listened as Captain Bevilacqua made another announcement:

"I'm happy to announce that we're back underway, and will be reaching full speed shortly. But due to today's delay, there's been a change in the ship's itinerary. We'll be bypassing our scheduled port of calls and arriving at our final destination, Naples, tomorrow on schedule. Those passengers headed for Nice or Genoa will be re-routed to our sister ships that sail local Mediterranean routes.

We're sorry for any inconvenience this may cause, so we'd like to offer free drinks to all passengers in the ballroom this evening.

Thank you for traveling on Mussolini's luxury flagship, the *SS Rex. Viva l'Italia! Viva Il Duce!*"

Oh no, I'm out of time, Josephine thought. *The murderer will get away when we reach Naples. I've failed.*

Chapter 18 - Vesuvius

The Bay of Naples must have been a beautiful sight in Roman times. Now it was like most big cities, sprawling outward from the historic city center, a mass of villas, apartment blocks and slums spreading like a giant octopus's tentacles grabbing the coastline away from the beautiful blue-green sea.

The old port was full of bobbing fishing boats of all shapes and sizes, moored to white and blue buoys, with nets rolled up at the ready.

"No one's going out to sea today," said Donato, who was standing at the railing with Josephine, Saltzie, Dominick, Maria, Antonio, Henrietta and Olivia. "Vesuvius looks like it's going to erupt and the winds are changing."

"Look!" Josephine pointed to the orange and red flaring lava spewing from the summit of the volcano overshadowing the city. "It's like fireworks!"

"But not so pleasant," said Dominick, "if those sparks hit you."

Plumes of sulfuric gases popped from holes in the ground in the Campi Flegrei hot fields in the city outskirts, creating a golden haze around the city. Naples seemed to be a cauldron of fire.

"It smells," said Saltzie, "and the city looks run down. I was expecting something more beautiful."

"Naples has its charms," said Donato. "It's a very ancient city. Let's go ashore, and I'll show you some of the sights. We can ride the funicular to the top of Vesuvius, if you dare."

There was a rumbling from Vesuvius, as if in response. It had another mild eruption, sending a spray of sparks and lava flying from its caldera. Then it was quiet.

"Vesuvius is putting on a show for our American guests," laughed Donato. "Don't worry, this is just another day in the life of the citizens of Naples."

"I'm not sure I like it," said Josephine.

"Are you frightened?" chided Lady Montague, who came alongside with Lady Capulet, dressed in chic suits and hats. "There's nothing to worry about. Vesuvius hasn't exploded in thousands of years, since Pompeii and Herculaneum were destroyed. That was 79 AD! Come on Gisella. The two of us aren't scared. We're so happy to be back home. We're going to ride the funicular to the summit to take in the view."

The ladies strode down the gangplank and headed into the city.

An ambulance arrived at the pier to take Romeo and Friar Lawrence for check ups. Romeo was protesting that he was fine, but the Guardia convinced him to go to the hospital. The nurse jumped in after them, and they sped off.

Cardinal Schlummer, La Bella Figura and Fernando Delitto were also preparing to debark. They came towards Josephine's group to say goodbye.

"It's shocking that Father Della Pietra killed Freda, Dr. Mahlberg and Isabella Schiavone, and that we'll never know who tried to poison Romeo and Friar Lawrence," Fernando said. "I doubt the Italian police will even bother to investigate."

"Yes, shocking," added the cardinal. "But I'm sure a higher justice will prevail." He looked up at the sky.

Josephine's friendly porter arrived, carrying the ornamental relic box, and stood ready with all the cardinal's copious luggage.

Cardinal Schlummer took the box and said goodbye.

Josephine's eyes followed him as he entered the veranda and started to descend the ship's grand staircase, carefully holding the relic box. *Mother Cabrini's relics,* she thought. *She was good to me when I was an orphan. If it wasn't for her, I wouldn't have had the courage to become a doctor.*

She said a prayer of thanks, then crossed herself.

She looked to the shoreline, down at the dock, where a group of Blackshirts were waiting to greet La Bella Figura, the cardinal and other dignitaries.

Then she noticed the green sea waves hitting the sand under the gangway.

A seagull fluttered low, but squawked and flew away. Small clouds of gas were lifting from the waters.

"Are the waters always so polluted?" she asked Donato.

"No, but the volcano's been active, with hot lava flowing into the sea. The smell is terrible when this happens."

Josephine reflected for a moment on the scientific principles of volcanoes and lava. She also watched the cardinal's procession and kept looking at the relic box. She remembered that Mother Cabrini liked to watch the seagulls from the orphanage window.

"That's it!" Josephine suddenly exclaimed. "Donato, Dominick, stop Cardinal Schlummer!"

Donato and Dominick raced down the grand staircase. They each grabbed an arm of the cardinal and pulled him back into the lobby.

Josephine came running down the staircase. Saltzie, and the others followed her.

"Cardinal Schlummer, I'm making a citizen's arrest. You killed Freda, Dr. Mahlberg and Isabella Schiavone."

"That's preposterous. Why would I do that?"

"Open that box," she commanded.

Donato grabbed the box from the cardinal's hands, despite his protests. He opened it and looked inside.

"There's only some bones here." He picked one up.

Josephine took the box. "I'm sorry Mother Cabrini," she said, as she pulled out the bones carefully, then shook the box.

"Ah ha!" she exclaimed, then felt around the edges of the inside. Her fingers found a spring lever, and the false bottom snapped open.

Inside were two rows of six vials, the size of perfume bottles. She picked one out. It had solids floating in a liquid, just like her jar experiment.

"Just as I thought," she said. "This is poison."

"Belladonna?" Saltzie asked.

"Not only Belladonna," Josephine began, "but something even worse. See these blue-green floating solids. That's sea algae."

"What do you mean?" asked Donato. "Sea algae is very common."

"When the sea heats up from lava flow, algae blooms grow Cyanobacteria. That produces a dangerous gas. It's called Cyanotoxin. I remember reading an article about it from an 1890's medical journal."

"She's always reading medical journals," Dominick said, "even in the car."

"Cyanotoxin is more deadly than mustard gas and kills almost immediately. There were reports of a man riding a horse along the beach, and the horse collapsed right out from under him. The man and his horse both died from the poison gas."

"Cyanotoxin?" asked Saltzie. "Is that what knocked me out from Juliet's poison bottle?"

"Yes, I believe so. We'll have to test for it, but I'm sure it must be deadly Cyanotoxin. Cyanotoxin is colorless with a suffocating, rotten egg odor, too."

"But if it's a gas, isn't it hard to use before it dissipates?"

"True, the gas is difficult to transport. It's heavier than air. Under pressure or exposed to heat, the containers may rupture and explode." She paused.

"So how can it be used as a murder weapon?"

"There's a solution to that problem. Cyanotoxin dissolves in a liquid. That's why it was suspended in poisonous Belladonna berry juice—to keep it stable. It was a brilliant plan. Two poisons, both extremely deadly, each supporting the other."

"A sinister plan," added Saltzie.

Josephine turned to Cardinal Schlummer. "What were you going to do with such a deadly gas?"

"I think I can answer that," said Ernesto, La Bella Figura. "Mussolini will invade Ethiopia any day now, and they'll face fierce resistance. But the Geneva Protocol of 1925 bans the use of mustard gas and other chemical and biological weapons. Cyanotoxin is lethal, but it's natural, as you say, and the gas would be untraceable after it dissipated."

"And Belladonna, even if found in the stomach, could be attributed to soldier's simply eating the wrong berries," Josephine added.

"Mussolini could wipe out thousands of soldiers and civilians resisting him, and no one would be the wiser."

"What a madman," Dominick said.

"Our great leader," said Cardinal Schlummer, "needs every advantage he can get. Naples can provide many canisters of Cyanotoxin from our sea algae gas, suspended in Belladonna. My experiments in American labs proved it worked."

"Your experiments?" Dominick asked.

"I'm a scientist, like Dr. Reva."

"You're not a cardinal?"

He snorted.

"But why did you kill Freda, Juliet? She had nothing to do with this."

"She killed herself. She wanted to try the poison to see how it worked. She thought a mild dose would put her into a short sleep, and it would be perfect for her role."

"I don't believe you," said Dominick. "A pity she's dead and can't answer for herself anymore."

"But why kill Dr. Mahlberg and Isabella Schiavone?"

"I didn't kill them." Cardinal Schlummer looked directly into Josephine's eyes.

"What about the attacks on Romeo and Friar Lawrence?"

"I had nothing to do with that."

"And what about the fascist groups in Brooklyn—are you their contact?"

"No."

Strangely, Josephine believed him.

The ship's officers led the cardinal away to the brig. Donato handed the relic box to Ernesto Cacciavolpe, because they were now on Italian soil.

The porter rushed over to Josephine, asking for her autograph. "You did it again, Miss Poison Femme Fatale!"

"Do you think the Devil's Advocate knew about this plot?" Saltzie interrupted.

"No. I think the cardinal asked Father Della Pietra to hear his confession. Then the priest was bound to secrecy. He couldn't say anything, even to save himself."

"And do you believe Cardinal Schlummer when he said he didn't kill Dr. Mahlberg or Isabella, or attack the others?"

"Yes," said Josephine. "I think there are two murderers, at least."

She walked over to Lord Montague and Lord Capulet. "Do you want to tell them, or should I? Dr. Porter-Graves saw Dr. Mahlberg's files."

They both heaved a sigh.

"I'm not Freda's father," said Lord Capulet. "Salvatore, Lord Montague, is."

"We didn't want anyone to know," said Lord Montague. "But when Freda wanted to marry Alberto, her own half-brother, we needed to stop it."

"I only found out during the cruise, when Bella, Lady Montague, told me she'd found out from Dr. Mahlberg. He discovered that I was sterile from an examination."

"Of course, Gisella, Lady Capulet already knew the truth. She'd had an affair with me."

"But our wives wouldn't let us tell the children. They thought it was better to try to end their relationship."

"But that wasn't working. Freda and Alberto were determined to marry."

"Dr. Mahlberg said it was our duty to tell our children. That genetics, well, if they married and produced offspring, it would interfere with us becoming a pure race of Italians."

"So you killed Dr. Mahlberg?" asked Josephine.

"No," said both opera dons. "We only went to talk to him. We struggled, then fought, and he fell over the railing and hit his head below. Then he fell overboard. We couldn't do anything about it."

"But his stomach contents were full of Belladonna berries," Josephine said. "Someone poisoned him first."

"And Isabella, too," Saltzie added.

Josephine paused to look out towards the city. She could just make out Lady Capulet and Lady Montague heading for the funicular.

"Your wives," pointed Josephine. "They were trying to poison you during the card game! Maria and Antonio told me that Isabella happened by during your game of Briscola, and took a handful of fruit. Perhaps that fruit was meant for you, Lord Capulet."

"My wife did suggest that I eat the darker fruit because it is sweeter."

"The power of suggestion," said Josephine. "That would explain why Isabella took the darker Belladonna berries before anyone else could. She was greedy and ate them first. I think Friar Lawrence and Romeo must have helped themselves to the fruit bowl, too."

"How do we call them back?" asked Dominick.

The group started waving from the ship. Donato ran to sound the ship's bellowing horn.

Josephine took Saltzie's binoculars. "They've stopped to look back at us," she said. "But now they've turned and are heading into the funicular."

The group watched as the funicular slowly climbed to the top of Vesuvius. The volcano was exploding in small gaseous clouds of sulfuric acid and fireworks of lava.

The *SS Rex* repeatedly sounded its foghorn.

Josephine pointed to the summit.

"Vesuvius is erupting! The coronet is imploding!" she exclaimed, watching through the binoculars. "Lava is spewing out."

People on the funicular looked like they were screaming, and when it stopped at the summit, they began fleeing down the volcano. But two figures remained.

It was Lady Montague and Lady Capulet. Josephine watched them through the binoculars, but there was nothing she could do.

The ladies grasped each other's hand, and then with a distant look back towards Josephine and the others on the ship, they bowed and waved, as if just finishing a performance.

Then they jumped into the flaming caldera.

Chapter 19 - Blackshirts

"Three beautiful opera divas are dead. Their voices silenced forever," said Josephine.

"But they were evil Fascists," said Saltzie, sipping an espresso on the ship's lower deck.

"Dr. Mahlberg, a Nazi sympathizer, and Isabella Schiavone, a fascist fashion designer, who stupidly got in the way."

"Cardinal Schlummer imprisoned for murder—do you really think Mussolini will sentence him?"

"I doubt it. His Cyanotoxin sea algae is useful to them. I hope La Bella Figura can figure out a way to conveniently "lose" those vials, and extradite the cardinal."

"At least we've solved the case for Chief Detective O'Malley. Or rather, you've solved it, Joe. You've done it again!"

They clinked their espresso cups.

The Porter-Graves were catching an early ferry to Capri. Henrietta repeated her invitation to Josephine, Saltzie, Dominick, Maria and Antonio.

"You can spend the day in Naples, then catch the evening ferry to Capri. I'll have dinner waiting," she said. "I can't wait to hear all the details."

The friendly porter and his pals arranged for all their luggage to be loaded on the evening ferry.

Josephine and her friends walked down the gangplank and into the cacophony that was Naples.

"We'va time before we return to New York," said Maria. "We coulda go shoppin'."

"You two go on ahead. I'd like to find some pharmacies and see what Italian medicines and homeopathic remedies are like," said Josephine.

She spotted Captain Bevilacqua at the helm of the ship's tender, starting the engine.

"Captain, where are you going?" she called.

"Two deaths on my ship, and two attempted murders. My career is over. *Me ne frego*, I don't give a hoot! I'm joining the navy!" he yelled back, waving his cap, and sped off around the point.

Dominick and Donato headed into town, Maria and Antonio went shopping, and Josephine and Saltzie decided to get a snack. The group agreed to meet later at the ferry dock for Capri.

At a pizzeria alongside the water, Dominick and Donato were passing the time, drinking wine and eating.

"Why is Neopolitan pizza so good? " Dominick asked.

"It's the water and the flour—it's got a special flavor from the volcanic ash."

There was a sound of breaking glass. Blackshirts were on the prowl, smashing shop keepers' windows.

Two Blackshirts came over to Dominick and Donato.

They stopped in front of their table and glowered.

"*Siete inscritti al Partita fascista?* Are you members of the Fascist Party?"

"Huh?" said Dominick. "What's a *Partita*? We're Americans, *americani*." He spoke slowly enunciating the words as if he didn't know any Italian.

Donato also adopted English to confuse the Blackshirts and buy some time. "Do you know where Vesuvius is?"

"Vesuvius," said a Blackshirt, and pointed up to the volcano.

"Why are you here?" The first Blackshirt asked. "What's your business?"

"We're on holiday," said Donato.

"Holiday? The two of you together? What are you miscreants, lovers?"

"No—"

"These two, they're lovers," the Blackshirt shouted in Italian. "Foreigners. Let's beat them."

He blew a whistle. Two more Blackshirts rushed over, and Donato and Dominick realized they were surrounded.

They were just about to dive into the sea to escape, when Ernesto, La Bella Figura approached, dressed in Blackshirt and carrying the cardinal's box with its glass vials filled with Cyanotoxin.

"These gentleman are my guests," said Ernesto. "They've brought a special liqueur from America. I'd be honored if you'd try some."

"Green color," said one Blackshirt, examining a vial. "It Abysinthe."

"Yes, Abysinthe," said Donato. "Here, take our glasses. There's not enough for everyone, so you drink it."

Ernesto poured the cardinal's liquid for each Blackshirt.

"*Il Duce*, Mussolini," the Blackshirts toasted, and swallowed their drinks.

"How long will this take?" Dominick whispered.

"About ten minutes," Ernesto answered quietly. "That's my boat at the end of the pier. The one with the flag. Here's the key. I just filled the tank."

"And you?" Dominick asked.

"Don't worry about me," Ernesto whispered. "They think I'm one of them. I was going to dump this liquid and replace it with something less toxic. This has saved me the trouble."

"Americans, *americani*," said one Blackshirt. "You tell Roosevelt that Mussolini good, good man."

"Okay, we'll be sure to do that," said Dominick. "Mussolini good, FDR bad. We get it. Here, drink some more."

The Blackshirts drank another round. Soon enough, they started to keel over.

One made several attempts to swing a punch, but seeing double, his swing fell short. Dominick easily avoided his fist.

The Blackshirts slumped over. Dominick and Donato said goodbye to Ernesto, and ran down the pier. They escaped into his boat and sped off.

* * *

At a caffé, two blackshirts sat down to eat next to Saltzie and Josephine's table. Staring at Saltzie, they began pointing at him.

Josephine suggested they pay and leave quietly.

"Halt! *Arrettevi*, give us your papers."

Josephine and Saltzie reluctantly gave over their passports.

"Saltzman, that's a Jewish name. A man who sells salt."

"No, for goodness sake. I don't sell salt. I'm a doctor. Gastro, you know, your rear end." He pointed to the soldiers' buttocks. "If you need any help down there, you need only ask."

"Down there? What do you mean by that?" The Blackshirt was visibly angry and started shouting.

"And you?" The other Blackshirt gestured towards Josephine. "What kind of purse is this. No woman carries such a thing." He grabbed her medical kit, unlatched it, and pulled out a catheter.

"I'm a medical doctor," Josephine said. "Get your hands off my instruments. You'll contaminate everything."

"A doctor? Why aren't you at home with your children?

"Because I don't have any children. Give me back my bag." Josephine began tugging at her satchel. The Blackshirt laughed and released it.

"A Jew and a female doctor—*incredibile*, incredible!" He smirked and blew a whistle. Other Blackshirts surrounded the pair.

"You're both under arrest. You can explain this absurdity to the head of the *Fasci di Combattimento*."

Saltzie scanned the harbor, searching for a way out of their predicament.

He spotted a lone boat at the far end of the pier.

He whispered to Josephine. "Like our prison break, but my car is at the end of the dock."

"I'm with you!"' She snatched the passports out of the Blackshirt's hands.

With a large sweep, Saltzie upended the table, sending food flying into the faces of the Blackshirts, spattering their black uniforms. He quickly grabbed a chair and held it legs pointed outward, fending off the Blackshirts with fencing moves. He stopped to land a strong upper cut to one of the Blackshirt's jaw, knocking him into the water.

"I learned that in The Tombs, that's prison," he shouted.

Josephine summoned her strength and pushed the other Blackshirts from behind, and Saltzie swung again, knocking the next two into the water like falling dominoes.

Another Blackshirt ran up beside Josephine, stooping to pull his friends out of the water. Josephine, on an adrenaline rush, swung her heavy medical bag, hitting him hard across the head and knocking him into the water, too.

"Run, Joe!" Saltzie shouted. They raced to the end of the dock and jumped into the motorboat. Saltzie hot-wired it, and they sped off.

"Good thing I used to steal joyrides at Coney Island," Saltzie winked and put his arm around Josephine.

"Even more I didn't know about you," she laughed.

"Steady now, we've got company." He pointed to a speedboat approaching, then another with its tricolor flag flying.

"Oh no, not more Blackshirts! They're like black flies," Josephine said. "What'll we do? We can't outrun them."

The flagged speedboat suddenly veered and cut in front of the other boat, sending it off course and into a pile of rocks. The Blackshirts were pitched overboard.

"We should help them," Josephine began, grabbing her medical kit.

"Not on your life. They were trying to arrest us. Don't worry about them, they're not your patients."

He pointed towards the flagged motorboat speeding towards them. It easily overtook their boat, then slowed alongside.

"Thought you could use the help!" Dominick called from the boat, and Donato waved from the wheel.

"Let's head back to the ship," Donato said. He pointed towards the army of Blackshirt patrol boats racing to retrieve their comrades.

"But I've got to scatter my mother's ashes in the Bay of Naples," said Josephine. "I've brought them all this way."

"You want to do it here?"

"No, not with those Blackshirts swimming about," she said. "Let me find a better place." She pulled out the chart of the Bay of Naples from the boat's pilot house.

"Where are we headed?" Dominick called.

Saltzie pointed to a tall rock at the end of the far point.

"How about that island?"

Josephine studied the chart.

"That's Capri," she said. "Perfect! Let's head to Mrs. Porter-Graves' villa."

Chapter 20 - Capri

A t dawn, Josephine and Saltzie hiked up to Anacapri, the beautiful village at the pinnacle of the island. The sun was rising, casting a purple haze above the water, and the white stones of the Roman villas were glowing a pink hue.

"One thing this voyage has proven," Saltzie said, "is that life is fleeting."

"Yes, that's true," said Josephine. "We must do all the good we can, before it's over."

"Sometimes, it's better to do good things together. Like our detective work on the Belladonna poisonings."

"Well, I'm the one who figured out that it wasn't only Belladonna, after all."

"But I'm the one who found the cufflink, and saved you from the cardinal and from those Blackshirts."

"I pulled myself up over the ship's rail and tied up the Devil's Advocate, and I knocked that Blackshirt in the water!"

"Oh, for Pete's sake, Josephine," Saltzie got down on one knee, "will you marry me?"

He pulled out the diamond and sapphire ring.

"Who's Pete?"

They both laughed.

"Josephine, we're on a peaceful island, surrounded by gorgeous blue-green sea, and it's a beautiful sunset. What could be more romantic than this?"

"I suppose," she said, remembering Maria's not so subtle pushes. "But I'm going to keep my professional name."

"Is that your only condition?"

"Yes," she laughed, "yes, it is."

"Remember when I told you six years ago that I'd be back for you?"

"Wasn't that after Chief Detective O'Malley released us from prison after the Aconite murders? I remember you said something in Latin."

"*Omnit vincit amor*, love conquers all."

"It's *omnia vincit amor*," Josephine couldn't resist correcting him. She finished Virgil's famous poem: *"et nos cedamus amori*, let's, too, yield to love."

They embraced and kissed passionately. He slipped the ring on her finger.

Maria and Antonio were delighted to hear the news. "Donato canna marry you when we're a back on te ship," Maria said. "He's officially *Capitano* now."

"Let's head down to the Blue Grotto, *La Grotta Azzurra*, to celebrate," Olivia said. "It's absolutely gorgeous. The water is a magnificent blue. We can take a swim before lunch."

"The grotto is where Tiberius and other emperors swam with their lovers," Donato said with a wink. "I'll show you their secret chamber. Dominick, are you coming?"

"Wouldn't miss it," Dominick laughed, and grabbed towels.

"But we didn't bring swimsuits," Josephine said.

"Who needs swimsuits?" laughed Olivia, taking the arms of both Dominick and Donato.

Josephine's eyes met Saltzie's. "You know, the grotto is 150 meters deep. The phosphorescent blue glow is caused by the refraction of sunlight through the grotto's surface opening, and a deeper submerged opening."

"Let's see if we can find that."

The two smiled, joined hands and followed the others down the rocky path.

Later that afternoon, after a delicious lunch of freshly caught seafood, Josephine and her friends were resting on the Porter-Graves' terrace. Looking across the bay towards Sorrento and Napoli, Josephine wondered where her mother's house was? *So many villas, it could be any one of them.*

"Did you ever get an address?" Saltzie asked.

"No, it was so long ago. Please hand me your binoculars."

Josephine scanned the coastline. But her gaze found Blackshirts arriving by boat in the harbor below.

"When Mussolini invades Abyssinia, there'll be no turning back."

"Any day now. They're like rabid dogs," Donato said. "Then Italy will become a belligerent, and I won't be able to transport any Americans aboard my ship. You'd best leave on the next sailing for New York tomorrow."

"But that's too soon—not before I find my mother's home."

"Dearest, Joe," said Saltzie, "I'm sorry, but if we go back into a city full of Blackshirts, we may not make it out alive. That's a risk I'm not willing to take."

"Yes, of course. You'd be in grave danger."

Josephine remembered what Sir Lucian had said. Mussolini would need to form an alliance with Hitler after antagonizing the League of Nations with his invasion of Ethiopia. She realized it was only a matter of time before the fascists would turn against the Jews, like the Nazis wanted.

Saltzie touched her cheek. "Let's scatter your mother's ashes and say goodbye."

Josephine, Saltzie, Maria, Antonio, and Henrietta, with Olivia leaning on the arms of Dominick and Donato, gathered on a ledge overlooking the ocean.

Josephine stepped forward and removed the top of the funerary urn.

"I hope you're proud of me, mamma. *Mi manci tantissimo*, I miss you so much." She poured her mother's ashes into the sea.

Saltzie put his arm around her shoulders.

* * *

That evening, the air was stifling hot from Vesuvius' eruption, so the group went for another descent to *La Grotta Azzurra*. They sat on the cool stone ledges, draped in towels, and drinking the fruits of Bacchus, like emperors of ancient times.

They stared into the unearthly blue depths.

"But the mystery's not fully solved," said Olivia. "Who was the fascist leader in Rome? Who was pulling the opera divas' and dons' strings, like a puppeteer?"

"Here's a possible answer," said Josephine, as she took a sip of wine. "It was Ernesto Cacciavolpe, La Bella Figura. He sent the opera stars to Brooklyn and instigated the plan to flush out American fascists. But he didn't know that Juliet would die, or that his actions would incite murder."

The group was silent, watching the soothing blue light playing on the grotto's stone walls.

Dominick spoke up. "I can't wait to get back to Brooklyn and report to Chief Detective O'Malley. We've stopped those fascists and destroyed their deadly poison weapon."

"But it's a shallow victory—we can't stop Mussolini from invading Abyssinia," Josephine said. "It's only the calm before the storm."

Her hand stirred the azure waters into a whirlpool, and the strange effect of the light's refraction coated the ripples in metallic silver.

"Spears, guns, submarines," she sighed, as the cave's light turned darker.

"Whether emperors and their legions, kings and their knights, or dictators and their foolish followers—war is a repeat performance."

The others nodded, then dove into the crystalline waters for a last swim.

Thank you for reading!

We hope you enjoyed BELLADONNA, Bitter Conduct.
Please leave a review *on your favorite sites,*
and recommend the series to others.

SOLIS MUNDI

ORDER MORE DR. JOSEPHINE PLANTAE PARADOXES
www.lmjorden.com
https://www.amazon.com/author/l.m.jorden/

ACONITE Queen of Poisons, a Roaring 20's Mystery
Based on a true story
It's the Roaring 20's, and a feisty orphan rises from the slums to become a doctor. Josephine Reva, Homeopath M.D., hangs her shingle in Brooklyn as the area's first woman doctor. If that isn't hard enough, Josephine's loyalty to the Hippocratic Oath will be tested under Prohibition, she's fighting for women's equality, and she won't give up her botanical poison cures.

Murder intrudes when a man is found dead from Aconite, a purple flower known as the *Queen of Poisons*. The Chief Detective suspects Josephine, and they begin a cat and mouse chase. Josephine must race to prove her innocence, and goes undercover as a flapper to spy. But complications arise when she falls for a debonair suspect.

Can Josephine unmask the killer? Can she follow her heart and save her career, while hiding her own dark secrets?

BELLADONNA Bitter Conduct, a 1935 Mystery Voyage
An Italian opera star spouts strange verses and collapses during the final act of Romeo and Juliet. Dr. Josephine Reva is in the audience and rushes to render aid. She believes the soprano was poisoned by Belladonna, a plant with deadly black berries.

Meanwhile, the Chief Detective uncovers plots to overthrow President Franklin D. Roosevelt. Could these events spark another World War? Josephine enlists her friends to follow the opera stars and spy on the high seas.

Who's the killer aboard the luxurious SS Rex? A shocking surreal artist, an avant-garde fashionista, a cardinal and priest carrying the relics of an American saint, a mysterious Mussolini official, a British lord, a Nazi doctor, or any of the narcissistic opera divas and dons?

Also along is a handsome paramour—is romance on the horizon for Josephine, if she can survive the trip?

Josephine must hurry to solve these Belladonna crimes with deeper roots, before the ship docks in Fascist Italy and it's too late.

CINCHONA Coney Island Bones, a 1941 Mystery
As Pearl Harbor draws America into another World War, a grave from long ago is dug up on Coney Island. The bones are almost

demolished in the name of progress, but Josephine and an archaeologist must put aside their differences to find out what happened. Alongside the skeleton are several strange artifacts.

Josephine must use her brilliant powers of deduction and her knowledge of medicinal plants to solve this paradoxical crime. The message from these Coney Island bones will have deeper implications for Josephine and her country.

GELSEMIUM, Memoir of a First Woman Doctor
In early 1900's New York, an Italian aristocrat falls on hard times, and struggles to protect her children as the Spanish Flu grips the city. Help arrives from an unexpected source, and her young daughter, Josephine, finds a way to save her family and realize her dream of becoming a first female doctor against the odds.

DIGITALIS Garden of Death
Chief Detective O'Malley lovingly tends his deceased wife's garden in her memory, but one day he finds an invasive and highly poisonous plant among the blooming varietals. He needs help from Dr. Josephine Reva, Homeopath MD, expert in botanical poisons, to find out who added the poison to his garden and why.

HELLEBORUS Death on the Hudson
An untimely horrific death on a river boat cruise leaves Dr. Josephine Reva, Homeopath MD, wondering: which botanical poison is the murder weapon disguised as a remedy, and which of the passengers administered the deadly dose?

ORDER HERE: www.lmjorden.com

L.M. JORDEN

Historical Notes

History should be tended like a flowering plant—water it from the roots, and it will bloom with many bright petals.

This work of fiction is based upon the life of the author's grandmother, Dr. Josephine Rera, M.D. (1903-1987), the first woman doctor in Borough Park and Bensonhurst, Brooklyn. She received a special commendation from the American Medical Association for fifty years' of service, and practiced medicine in Brooklyn for over six decades.

To reconstruct the past is no easy task, especially for a historical series such as the Dr. Josephine Plantae Paradoxes, which weaves in a larger than normal amount of history. As William Faulkner wrote, "The past is never dead. It's not even past" in *Requiem for a Nun*. It's no wonder we're reliving some of the same paradigms over and over again.

Fascism, as many historians note, is a state-controlled corporatism, brutally enforced by violence and hatred, with a suspension of civil liberties. The frightening appeal of its ideology continues today. In 1934, Congressional testimony from Marine Corps Major General Smedley Butler showed the existence of the fascist-inspired "Wall Street Putsch", also known as the "Business Plot" alleging that some business leaders planned a coup d'état to overthrow President Franklin Delano Roosevelt. This event is now almost completely forgotten, but it showed how Americans came perilously close to supporting fascist ideology in 1933. (McCormack-Dickstein Committee 1934-1935 and Congressional records INVESTIGATION OF NAZI PROPAGANDA ACTIVITIES AND INVESTIGATION OF CERTAIN OTHER PROPAGANDA ACTIVITIES PUBLIC HEARINGS BEFORE THE SPECIAL COMMITTEE ON UN-AMERICAN ACTIVITIES, HOUSE OF

REPRESENTATIVES SEVENTY-THIRD CONGRESS SECOND SESSION AT Washington, D.C. December 29, 1934 HEARINGS No. 73-D-C-6).

Even after Kristelnacht, the pro-Nazi American Bund organized a rally at Madison Garden on February 20, 1939, with over 20,000 supporters. "We need be in no doubt as to what the Bund would do to and in this country if it had the opportunity," *The New York Times* wrote in an editorial later that week. "It would set up an American Hitler." https:// timesmachine.nytimes.com/timesmachine/1939/02/22/issue.html

The Brooklyn Public Library collection contain an original pamphlet well worth viewing about 1930's fascist meetings held in Brooklyn and Long Island. In November 17-18 of 1934, a meeting was held by Friends of the New Germany, a fascist national group, with members coming from all over the country, and Brooklyn received mention at the top of the list as the "seat of the leadership district." The New World Telegram on August 12, 1935 estimated there were 1100 Nazis in Ridgewood, Brooklyn alone, and an article appeared on August 14, 1935 saying the Nazis offered "extensive programs of social and athletic activities." In addition, there was a summer camp in Yaphank, Long Island which attracted an estimated 3000-5000 members each weekend; it was decried by a local town representative.

Prior to World War II, there was growing Nazi and Fascist sentiment in Brooklyn and throughout the New York area, and many brave New Yorkers opposed it. On April 23, 1938 Charles Weiss, the editor of a Brooklyn anti-Nazi magazine, was found beaten with swastikas etched on his back. He worked in the offices of the Anti-Communist Anti-Fascist and Anti-Nazi League at 130 Flatbush Avenue. On March 13, 1938 Brooklyn's long-serving Representative Emmanuel Celler appeared on a radio program in which he stated his alarm at the spreading of Nazi ideology. https:// www.bklynlibrary.org/blog/2013/02/22/nazism-1930s-brooklyn.

The Missionary Sisters of the Sacred Heart, led by Mother Frances Cabrini, founded Columbus Hospital in 1892 with the aim of serving rich and poor patients alike, an idea that was revolutionary for its time. The miracle in this novel's prologue is drawn from the historical records. Mother Cabrini died in 1917. After the miracles, the process of her veneration quickly began in 1928. She was venerated by the Roman Catholic Church in 1933, beatified in 1938 and sanctified in 1947 as the first American saint. She is known as the Patron Saint of Immigrants.

The real Dr. Josephine Rera was a foundling and met Mother Cabrini in an orphanage. Dr. Rera often said it was that meeting that inspired her to become resolute in her goal of becoming one of the first woman doctors in Brooklyn, against the odds.

The characters of Cardinal Schlummer and the Devil's Advocate and their actions, and the relics in this book are entirely fictitious, and products of the author's imagination.

New York Homeopathic Medical College existed as a highly regarded institution in the Yorkville area of Manhattan, and the author's grandmother, Dr. Josephine Rera, graduated there in 1926 with an M.D.degree, the same year as our heroine, Dr. Josephine. The medical college (affiliated with Flower Hospital during Dr. Rera's studies) was founded by William Cullen Bryant ((1794-1878), a homeopathy devotee, abolitionist and noted Romantic poet and editor of the *New York Evening Post*. Bryant Park, next to the New York Public Library, is named in his honor. NYHMC is now New York Medical College, located in Valhalla, NY. The New York City College of Homeopathic Medicine is entirely fictional. The "Yorkvillains" classmates are entirely fictionalized in the novel. Their behavior would be considered offensive in the #Me,too generation, but similar experiences were reported by my grandmother and other female medical students during the 1920's.

The *Brooklyn Daily Eagle* began publishing in 1841 and was once edited by Walt Whitman. It went out of business in 1955. There is a newer

Brooklyn Eagle publishing since 1996, and the use of the older *Brooklyn Daily Eagle* in this novel is entirely fictionalized.

The US Neutrality Act was signed in July of 1935, with an exception granted for "cash and carry" in 1937, as American prepared for war.

Cyanotoxin,a deadly toxic substance found in blue-green algae, can occur naturally in marine areas. Interestingly, the Central Intelligence Agency considered developing a "poison pill" containing Saxitoxin, one of the most deadly and fast-acting poisons derived from shellfish. It causes nerve paralysis, similar to tetrodotoxin, a deadly poison in the Japanese blow fish. The destruction of such bacteriological weapons was ordered in 1969, following the signing of an international treaty, but certain poisons were later reported to still exist in laboratories.

Funiculì, Funiculà was a song composed in 1880 by Luigi Denza, with lyrics from Peppino Turco, perhaps as a joke to commemorate the opening of the first funicular on Mount Vesuvius. It is still popular today, and versions have been sung by opera stars Luciano Pavarotti, Andrea Boccelli, and others, including the Chipmunks.

There were several popular fascist songs about Mussolini's invasion of Ethiopia, including *La Faccetta Nera,* and many about Italians saving Abyssinian women and men. Some of these war songs would be now considered extremely racist and sexist. The songs sung about Abyssinia in this novel are entirely made-up.

A few interesting notes about birds: feathers on ladies' hats were in fashion through the 1920's, then stopped when journalists begin looking into the "feather trade". This feather trade was barbaric and wiped out entire flocks of beautiful birds, such as egrets, ibises and herons, and ostrich farms began appearing. Feathers came back in fashion with some alarm in the mid-1930's: who can forget that ostrich feather dress in the movie Top Hat? The movie was released in August of 1935, a month before Dr. Josephine Reva set sail in Belladonna, Bitter Conduct. Maria, Henrietta and Olivia, among many others during this time, would most likely have been donning real bird feather hats, unfortunately, but the author wanted to emphasize that there were many activists who were wearing faux feather hats in protest. https://www.saturdayeveningpost.com/2016/06/looks-kill-fashion-extinction/

A historical novel should engage in a reconstruction of the past, what Michel Foucault called "the archaeology of knowledge," see Michel Foucault, *The Archaeology of Knowledge* (A.M. Sheridan Smith trans., Pantheon Books 1972). This author, by staying faithful to the research, aimed to let many "voices of the past" speak, and to make this historical mystery an engaging story without omitting the turbulent events of the era.

L.M. JORDEN

Author

L. M. JORDEN is an award-winning journalist, author and retired professor of English and History. She holds the Master of Science from Columbia University Graduate School of Journalism, won a New York Press Association award, and lives in Europe and New England with her family, furry friends and lots of plants.

Her company, **World 3i,** specializes in global fact-checking and multilingual research.

www.lmjorden.com
https://www.amazon.com/author/l.m.jorden/
www.facebook.com/LMJorden/